escaping indigo
BOOK THREE

# scratch

# track

# ELI LANG

RIPTIDE
PUBLISHING

Riptide Publishing
PO Box 1537
Burnsville, NC 28714
www.riptidepublishing.com

Scratch Track

Cover art: Natasha Snow, natashasnowdesigns.com
Editor: May Peterson, maypetersonbooks.com
Layout: L.C. Chase, lcchase.com/design.htm

ISBN: 978-1-62649-691-0

First edition
January, 2018

Also available in ebook:
ISBN: 978-1-62649-690-3

escaping indigo

BOOK THREE

# scratch track

X

# ELI LANG

*For my parents.*
*I'd write out all the reasons why, but it'd take up the whole*
*page. Thank you for all the things.*

# TABLE OF
## contents

# chapter one

X

Sometimes, when I'm listening to music, it's like I'm standing in the middle of this whirlwind of sound, and it washes over me. Like I've fallen into the melody and it's everywhere, surrounding me and inside me. And it clicks something on, some switch in my mind or my heart, and for those few minutes, everything is *right*. Good. Like it makes sense. And nothing else matters.

Watching Escaping Indigo play was like that. I felt the same way about Rest in Peach, the band I was watching now, too. I'd seen them play live before, but this was different—now I was seeing them through the thick glass window of a recording studio, while they tracked a song and I stared from the other side of the soundboard. And I hadn't expected this—I hadn't known they were going to be here, and I hadn't been prepared to see them, any of them, again.

I turned to Bellamy, who was standing behind me, nodding along to the song. He had this contemplative look on his face, and I knew he wasn't only enjoying the music. He was picking it apart, figuring out why it had been put together that way, what was working and what wasn't, why those musical choices had been made. Bellamy was great on stage, better than almost any performer I'd ever seen, but putting songs together was where he was at home. He was made for recording. It was why he'd decided to try his hand at producing this album himself.

"You didn't tell me they were going to be here." I tried to keep my tone casual, like it was a nice surprise, but there were cracks in my voice, where the words came out tight.

Bellamy didn't seem to notice. Beside him, his boyfriend, Micah, took his hand and gave it a shake, bringing him back down.

Micah was carrying on his own conversation with Ava and Tuck, but part of his mind was always focused on Bellamy. It took Bellamy a minute to blink and come back out of whatever music-induced haze he'd been in.

"I didn't know." Bellamy turned to face me. "I knew we probably wouldn't be the only band here. It's a big studio. I didn't know who else it'd be, though." In the other room, the song came to an end. The band's singer, Ty, leaned into their mic and said hello to us. We waved and the rest of the band waved back.

I waved too, to the whole band. But my focus was on one person. Nicky. Sitting behind the drum set, his sticks held loosely in one hand on his knee. He was wearing a black tank top, and the tan skin over his collarbones and throat glistened. They'd been playing hard for a while. He was barefoot, and through the tangle of chords and stands, I could glimpse his long toes, where he was curling them into the plush red-and-gold rug. He always played barefoot. I remembered that about him from when we'd toured together. He'd had a pair of flip-flops he'd kick on and off, so he wouldn't step on anything sharp on the way to the stage.

He was watching me. Not trying to pretend he was simply looking in our direction, like I was trying to pretend I was casually looking in his. He wasn't casual about it at all. This was blatant. He kept staring, waiting for me to stare back. And when I did, he held my eyes, until I had to glance away again because I couldn't be so connected to him, even through two rooms and a sheet of thick glass.

Because when I saw him, I remembered how he'd looked when he'd been poised over me, my palm at the small of his back. Urging him on, rising up to meet him. The sound of our breaths, heavy and harsh in the dark. I remembered what it was like to be inside him, to be so close to him that, for those few hurried minutes, I'd forgotten where my body ended and his started, muscles and bones melting one into the other.

Ty was leaning toward the rest of their band now, waving back and forth between the drum set and the bass. I couldn't quite hear what they were saying—snippets came through on the microphone, but they were facing the wrong way. Nicky laughed and shook his head. He'd cut his hair—the last time I'd seen him, he'd constantly been pushing his brown bangs out of his eyes, but now it was too short for that. He was the same, otherwise, though. Tall and fit, smiling, confident. I could still picture the same smile on his face, when he'd curled up next to me in my bunk bed on the tour bus.

That was the last time I'd seen him. Rest in Peach had split off to start their solo tour right after, and we'd picked up different opening bands in each of the last few cities, to close out Escaping Indigo's tour. Nick and I had made vague plans to see each other again, to get together and maybe see where things went, but we never had. Or I never had. He'd called a couple of times, but by then everything around me had been falling apart, and I hadn't been in any place to call him back. I hadn't wanted to. I hadn't wanted anything like that.

Micah had left off his conversation with Ava. He still had Bellamy by the hand, but I didn't think either of them noticed they were doing it. Micah turned to me and raised his eyebrows. "You okay?"

"Uh-huh." I pushed my fingers back through my hair. It was a nervous gesture, but Micah wouldn't see that. We didn't know each other well enough to recognize each other's habits, even though he'd been my brother Eric's best friend for years.

I glanced back at Nick. He'd gotten Ty to laugh, and it looked like they were about to start up another song.

"They sound great," Bellamy mumbled, more to himself than anyone. I nodded back anyway.

I'd thought of Nick over the last year. I'd thought of him as the last truly good, free, easy thing to happen to me. Sometimes I'd gone back in my mind to that one night, had relived it and held it close as a comfort when things got too hard, too painful. But I hadn't ever thought of calling again. That time was past. I hadn't actually ever thought I'd see him again. I wasn't sure why—Rest in Peach and Escaping Indigo played the same venues, toured the same circuits. We were bound to run into each other. Maybe I'd figured I'd avoid him and that would be that. Or that maybe seeing him wouldn't feel like . . . so much. So much left unsaid and undone.

But now here we were. Watching each other. Or he was watching me. I could still feel his eyes on me, even though I was looking away. I hadn't expected this or been ready for it in any way. And no one else knew anything was wrong.

Maybe Micah did. He'd always been observant. He leaned over to touch his hand to my arm and said, "Ava said the rooms are ready for us upstairs, if we want."

I nodded. It hadn't been a very long trip—only a few hours up the coast. But getting all the gear packed and getting everybody ready to go—that, especially—had been exhausting. Tuck and Ava and Bellamy were good people, smart and talented, but getting them all to do one thing on time was like pulling teeth. And I was the one in charge of doing it, whenever it involved the band as a whole. Gently prodding and then cajoling until they got themselves together. I was glad now that they were staying in the house attached to the studio. It would make everything simpler.

I went with Micah and Tuck, and we gathered up suitcases and bags, and started hauling them upstairs. There wasn't actually any reason for me to be here, so I wanted to make myself as useful as possible. I'd driven the van with the trailer attached up to the studio, but that was it as far as my job went, really. I didn't have anything else to do, now that we were here, except make sure everyone was fed and in the studio on time. We weren't on tour, and this wasn't supposed to be work for me, so my duties were fuzzy.

The band was making a party out of it, in a way. Micah was here with Bellamy, and Ava's girlfriend Cara was flying out for a weekend to see her and sit in on the recording. Micah had asked, guilelessly, if I wanted to come along too, since they were planning it as more of a get-together than a serious job, and the rest of the band had jumped all over that idea. Saying it wouldn't be the same if I wasn't there. I hoped it was a good idea—I liked seeing them all happy, but recording was notoriously stressful. I'd be here to witness it firsthand, now.

I knew they could get along without me just fine, and having me tag along was mostly kindness. But I wanted to be with them instead of going home. Besides, I was curious.

While we walked through twisty hallways and up a couple of steep stairways to the main floor of the house, I was able to push Nick and Rest in Peach almost to the back of my mind. Tuck was grumbling about how heavy Ava's bag was—"I know she's not really into shoes. What the hell does she have in here?"—but I was distracted by the studio itself.

Escaping Indigo had recorded here once before, and Tuck had tried to tell me about this place, but words hadn't done it justice. I'd been in recording studios before, briefly, but Ben Ammondine Studios wasn't like any of those places. It was built into an old house, smack in the middle of a neighborhood outside of Los Angeles—that in itself wasn't odd. Lots of studios started out life as old houses. They grew out of necessity. But this one was mostly underground. The house was built into the side of a hill. Part of the back, the basement, and parts of the old garage were the studio, and it had been expanded so it extended for rooms and rooms, under the house.

That, and the two soundboards, meant there was plenty of room for more than one band to record an album at a time. Enough space that maybe I really could avoid Nicky while we were both here.

As soon as I thought it, I knew it would never happen. Escaping Indigo and Rest in Peach were all friends. They'd want to get together. And it would be weird if I avoided them.

Coming up from the closed-off, windowless recording studios into the brightly lit, many-windowed house was like emerging from another world. The hallway we stepped into was narrow, but it expanded into a decently sized kitchen, which was open to a large living room stuffed with couches. There was another hallway off the living room, and I could glimpse open doors, some leading into bedrooms at the back of the house.

I was pretty sure there weren't enough rooms in the actual house part for two bands to stay, though, despite the size of the studio underneath, but I asked Tuck, to double-check.

"No, it's just us staying here," he said, dropping his huge bag beside him. I couldn't imagine what he had in it. He was staying by himself. His girlfriend, Lissa, had decided to drive up for a few days later on, when Cara was here, instead of spending the whole time with us. "Most of Rest in Peach lives around here, so it's no big deal. I think Danni's staying with Ty. Or maybe she's getting a hotel."

"Expensive," I said, mostly to myself.

"Recording's expensive," he replied, and I couldn't argue with that. Everything about music was expensive. Worth it, though.

The owner of the studio, Ben, had given us three bedrooms. Ava had her own, there was one for Micah and Bellamy, and Tuck and

I were sharing. I wasn't sure what we'd do when Lissa came for the weekend, but I figured we'd make it work. The bedrooms were small but airy, the white walls and comfortable, modern furniture making the space seem as big and open as possible. And since they were at the back of the house, they had the illusion of being up high. The view was amazing: houses and little patches of yard, and streets in a tight grid pattern, laid out for miles and miles.

Tuck claimed a bed and flopped right onto it, his hand going immediately for his phone. I figured he was texting Lissa, but Ava was probably next on the list, even though she was right down the hall. Those two couldn't go five seconds without talking.

I left the room quietly, but Tuck probably didn't notice. Snooping wasn't really my plan. I just . . . wanted to look, wanted to *see* this place. So many records had been made here. So much creativity under one roof. So much modern history. I wandered my way down the hall. There were pictures on the walls. Like family portraits, in plain, boring black frames. I stopped and studied them, and saw that they were that history, captured and contained. Photos of musicians, with Ben or standing inside one of the several recording rooms. Bands I'd grown up listening to, bands I'd heard on the radio, bands whose albums I'd bought and played, over and over.

I kept walking, not paying as much attention to where I was going. It was . . . overwhelming. In a good way. But it was a lot to take in.

My wandering took me to the kitchen, which was as clean and white as the rest of the house. I hadn't expected all this . . . cleanliness, in a place where rock stars routinely hung out. The only concession to rock was the bright-purple toaster that sat on the counter. And the pictures pinned to the fridge. More bands, and flyers, and ticket stubs, and reminders about who was flying in when to record, and notations for which instruments to set up.

I wandered over to the kitchen window and gazed down, past the small garden in the front yard and the driveway gate to the road beyond. From the outside, this place didn't look like anything special, wasn't much different than any other house on the block.

Would Eric have liked it here? I wondered if it would have been what he'd expected, what he'd have wanted. I couldn't picture him here, or anywhere like it. Not in this upper part, these neat rooms, with these neatly framed pictures all through the house. I could imagine him in the basement rooms, though. I could picture him under those pale lights, guitar in his lap, talking with Ben about how a song should sound. When the drums should come in. How the vocals should be mixed. I could picture him bent over a notebook, scribbling down lyrics, getting inspired by everything he talked about with Micah. He would have loved that part.

Someone made a noise in the kitchen behind me, and I turned around to see Bellamy standing there. He stood almost awkwardly, his arms crossed over his chest, hands cupping his elbows tightly. It should be unusual to see that on him, uncertainty in a man who made his living being as bold and loud and extroverted as humanly possible. But when he wasn't on the stage, Bellamy was more reserved. This was his normal.

He still looked like something ethereal, standing in the golden evening light coming in through the window. All the blond highlights in his hair shone, and his skin glowed. He'd painted his nails a dark purple, almost black, and when he tapped the fingers of one hand against his elbow, the nails sparkled, the dull paint catching the sun. He would always look like a rock star, no matter what he did or how he dressed, or how introverted he got when he wasn't in the public eye.

I turned all the way around, putting my back to the window, and crossed to the island in the middle of the kitchen. He came over and pushed himself up onto one of the barstools lining one side. "I forgot. About you and Nicky. I'm sorry."

I shrugged and leaned forward, letting my elbows rest on the countertop. "You said you didn't know they'd be here."

"I didn't."

"So what are you apologizing for?"

He glanced down at his fingers and picked at a corner of one nail. "I asked you to come here with us."

I sighed. "Micah asked me, actually."

His eyes flicked up to meet mine. "We all wanted you here, Quinn."

"And I want to be here," I said, struggling for a casual tone. That was the thing. I *did* want to be here. And I *knew* they wanted me here too. I wanted a few weeks of listening to my friends make music, a few weeks where I got to see and hear the process of recording an album in the most intimate way possible. A few weeks where we partied and hung out and got excited about songs and the next tour. That was *my* normal.

But Nicky had thrown me off. I'd seen him and felt . . . so out of place. Like my world had tipped on its axis. Like I'd found myself on the outside, peering in, and everything I saw was just slightly distorted. It was ridiculous. We barely knew each other. We'd spent a few weeks touring the same venues, flirting endlessly, and then we'd spent the one night together, the culmination of all those heavy stares and brief touches. And that was it. It hadn't meant anything. It was only . . . that I'd liked him, and that the end of the tour had marked the worst and most important moment of my life. And now it was all tangled up in my mind.

"It's supposed to be fun, though," Bellamy said, bringing me back to the here and now. "Not . . . It's not supposed to be you trying to avoid an ex."

"He's not an ex," I replied, as gently as I could, trying not to snap out the words. "He was . . ." *A fling*, I wanted to say. *A fuck*. But I'd liked Nicky too much for either of those words. It had only been the one night that we'd slept together, but we'd also had all the days and nights before that too, when we'd gotten to know each other as people, maybe as friends. I didn't want to minimize that. "It didn't end up going anywhere. So. It's fine. It'll be fine. I'm not going to avoid him."

I hadn't quite made up my mind until I'd said it out loud, but it was true. Like I'd thought before, there was no real way to avoid him, anyway. And I didn't want to. "I'm going to pretend it didn't happen." I ran my hand back through my hair. "God, it was only one night. I didn't think you even knew about it."

Bellamy smiled. "I'm pretty observant."

I huffed out a laugh. That was true. But maybe I hadn't been very discreet, either. It wasn't that I'd been hiding it, exactly—either my attraction to Nicky, or who I was attracted to in general. It was that I didn't talk about it. There wasn't a ton of point. I didn't fall into lust for too many people. So it had always seemed simpler to keep it quiet.

Until ... I figured it all out for myself, maybe. Until I had labels I liked to describe it, so I could put it into words and not have to fumble around with it in front of my family or my friends.

But Escaping Indigo was family and friends wrapped up into one, and being on tour was ... freeing. Like I'd been let loose, and everything we did had this edge of unreality to it. So when we were out on the road ... I let go. I let myself ... want things and need things; I let myself be myself. And for a few weeks, a year ago, that had meant trying to seduce Nicky of Rest in Peach. And it had worked.

"Are you sure?" Bellamy was drawing a circle on the countertop with the tip of his finger now, but his eyes were on me, studying me.

"Sure of what?"

"Sure you don't mind? Sure you can pretend everything's fine?"

I didn't know what he was going to do about it if I said no. He couldn't exactly make Rest in Peach leave. If I wasn't sure, the only option I had was to leave myself. Or hide away in the room I was sharing with Tuck, but what would be the point?

"It'll be fine," I answered, and I tried to say it so we'd both believe it. "Everything *is* fine. What Nicky and I were doing together ... it's over."

He narrowed his eyes at me but nodded, and I hoped that would be enough.

I was saved from having to reassure him again, or explain anything, by the sound of footsteps coming up the stairs. A second later, I heard the door open, and Ben and all of Rest in Peach was coming into the kitchen to meet us. So it seemed I'd be testing that resolve right away.

There were hugs and handshakes all around. Bellamy knew Ben, of course, from when they'd recorded here before. He introduced me. I liked him pretty much immediately—he was intriguing, even in appearance. He was short and almost weedy looking. He had on a pair of glasses he kept pushing around his face, down his nose so he could peer over them, or right up onto his forehead when they got in the way. His hair flopped around his ears, and he was wearing a faded pair of unfashionable jeans and a short-sleeved button-down shirt, open over a plain black T-shirt. He was geeky in the best way, the exact type of person who'd put every technical aspect of your music right. But he was also covered in tattoos, which were a sharp contrast to his otherwise nerdy appearance. They snaked over his arms and down his hands, and there were some poking out of the collar of his shirt, climbing up his neck almost to his jaw.

Ben greeted me like I was another member of the band, not a hanger-on, and it endeared me to him. Then Ty came over with a huge smile on their face. I went to take their hand, but they shook their head and wrapped me up into a hug, rocking me back and forth. I laughed and hugged them back. Danni, who played keyboards, and Elliot, the bassist, said hello next. It was surprisingly good to see them again. I'd thought about them, sometimes, after that tour together. We'd played with a lot of bands, traveled with them, lived together, really. And we'd made quite a few friends. But Rest in Peach had been the most fun, the people we had seemed to click with, right away. I'd been following their music, listening to their newest album, but I'd missed *them*.

Nicky hung back. Ty herded Bellamy, Elliot, and Danni over to one side of the island. I wasn't sure if Ty knew, like Bellamy did, that Nicky and I had had a thing, or if they were simply that perceptive. They did it so smoothly it didn't seem manipulative at all, but it definitely gave me and Nick a little space.

"Hey." His voice was husky and rough, like I remembered.

"Hey." Oh, fuck me. I was definitely not who anyone went to for easy conversation at the best of times. It wasn't my skill, and right now, I was . . . nervous, I was pretty sure. I didn't usually get nervous—I was the guy who held it together for everyone else—and it had been a long time since I'd felt that emotion. It took me a second to figure out what it was. But it was tangling my tongue up and putting in some block where clever conversing skills were supposed to be.

But Nick smiled at me. Gently and vaguely self-deprecating. "This is going to be awkward, huh?"

It was almost the same thing Bellamy had asked, but it was different coming from Nicky while he was wearing that expression. It made me relax.

"Well," I said, reaching for a smile of my own, "the last time I saw you, you were . . ." I waved my hand through the air.

His eyes widened. "Oh, I remember. It would be hard not to."

That made me blush. I looked ridiculous when I blushed. I was too big and bulky for it. Blushes were for delicate people, like Bellamy or Micah. Or Nick. Then again, he wasn't exactly delicate. He was . . . willowy. Tall and tough and wiry from all the drumming. Like sea glass, polished to a fine roughness.

I was just rough.

Standing there, in the bright kitchen, feeling slightly grimy from all the loading and unloading of gear, and the travel, I wondered what it was Nicky had ever seen in me to begin with. I hadn't questioned it at the time, except to think that I was lucky to get his attention. But on the other hand . . . Nick had seemed to like what he saw. Like *me*. And that was all I'd wanted to focus on.

"I thought . . ." He took a deep breath, enough that I could see his chest rise and fall with it. That smile flickered, and instead of being slightly teasing, it looked almost pained. "I thought I might see you again. After, I mean. After that tour."

We'd talked about it. After we'd finally gotten over the flirting and into bed, and the panicky relief of finally having him so close had faded slightly, I'd realized I just liked the guy. We'd gotten along. He'd been fun to joke with and hang out with, and I'd enjoyed being around him. Rest in Peach had been going their own separate way for their tour, and Nicky and I had both known we hadn't had anything serious between us. Not then, at least. But I'd said I'd like to see him again, maybe call him up when we all got home.

But of course, I hadn't. Nicky had tried, and I guessed he'd asked Bellamy about me. But Bellamy wouldn't be sharing secrets if I didn't want those secrets known. And at the time, I hadn't been in any place to tell Nick—a guy I liked but, honestly, barely knew—all the things that were going wrong in my life.

"I'm sorry," I said now. "I didn't . . . I had stuff . . ." I still couldn't tell him. Not like this. Not here, in front of these people. It had taken me so long to tell the *band*. There was no way I could say it with all of Rest in Peach here. I wasn't sure if I wanted to tell Nick himself.

He waved his hand again. "It's fine. Really."

It didn't sound quite fine. His voice was a little tense, tight, like he was forcing the words out. But it was only a hint. And there wasn't anything I could do about it, as much as I'd like to.

Ty, who was apparently Captain Perceptive, drew us into the conversation then. A few minutes later, Ava, Tuck, and Micah came out to the kitchen, and the atmosphere went closer to party-like. Tuck suggested we all go out for something to eat, then come back and listen to the stuff Rest in Peach had recorded that afternoon.

It was a good idea, and it made everything easy, for me at least. We went out as a group, and there was always someone else to talk to, instead of only Nicky. Not that I didn't want to talk to him, but we didn't have to be alone together and making up conversation. I was surrounded by my friends, and they made everything simpler. Simpler and fun. That was how I wanted it. That was how I wanted this whole thing to go.

# chapter two

the first day of recording for Escaping Indigo was a weird mix of excitement, giddiness, and grueling work—for the band, not me, although it was hard not to float on whatever emotions they were putting out. I tried to savor it because I figured by the next day, the initial excitement would be wearing off and the grueling part would be what was left. The band would find its rhythm eventually, before our recording time was up. But they hadn't done this in a while, and it was all new, all over again. It was probably different for every album too.

"We agreed we'd do a double chorus there, instead," Tuck was saying. I was sitting on the couch in the back of the room, my legs curled up under me, watching them hash out the songs.

Bellamy shrugged. "I decided it doesn't work as well. We should go back and do a half bridge, then a chorus."

"That's insane. No one writes songs like that, Bellamy."

"We're not everyone else, Tuck," Bellamy retorted, voice just as dry.

Ava laughed, making the pinched lines of Tuck's face soften. I shook my head at all of them, but they weren't paying me any attention. Bellamy and Tuck had been writing songs for the new album for a while, since the last tour. Slowly—Bellamy was a perfectionist, and Tuck was always telling him to take it easy, so the process of writing had been . . . not leisurely, but mellow. Plus, Ava had spent a few weeks away with her family, so most of her drum stuff for the songs had been done across the country. I knew Bellamy wished they'd all had more time to practice the stuff together, but it had been good for Ava. She'd somehow found time to fall in love with a really awesome girl, and she seemed . . . more settled in herself. Like pieces of her had been loose and out of place before, and now they weren't.

But all of that meant the songs were still being created. The bones were there, but not the polish, so the band ended up pausing in the middle of songs and working stuff out. It was good, in a way—it would help them figure out exactly how they wanted things. Escaping Indigo was lucky—having a record deal meant the label paid for more recording time than the band could ever have afforded on their own. So there wasn't a huge rush to get everything done all at once. But time *was* still limited, so there was a lot of pressure for everyone.

I didn't have much to do, though. I'd helped them unload all the gear—and there was a lot. More than we toured with, it seemed. We'd piled the trailer and the old van high with guitars and drums and about ten thousand cymbals and keyboards and effect pedals, and anything else the band could think of. Ava had brought four snares, and I couldn't imagine that they all sounded that different from each other, but she swore they did. We set up a few things, and left the rest of the stuff in its cases for when they needed it. And then my job was basically done.

Ben, who was serving both as recording tech and semiproducer, said something about the guitar sound to Bellamy. Bellamy's face went tight while he tried to absorb the feedback, but he nodded. "We can try that," he said, swinging back around to Tuck and Ava. "Let's do it again."

Tuck nodded and started playing the intro. He was floating in music space, blissed out on the possibilities of what they were doing. Ava seemed to be drifting between that state and complete worry. She checked her phone a lot—Cara was probably texting her, to help her stay calm.

It was exciting for everyone. But it was also hour after hour of taking feedback on their personal creativity. While it was good for the band, and good for the music, it wore a person down. And since Bellamy was producing, he had to be in charge of final decisions. I knew he could do it, and he'd be good at it, once he got the hang of it. I wasn't sure he knew it yet, though. He wasn't used to playing that role.

In the middle of the afternoon, Ty and Danni came to see how it was going. They were recording with a different tech, and their own producer, but Ben kept running back and forth while the two bands worked, checking in, recording snippets, making sure everything was going okay. Rest in Peach must have decided to call it a day, though. I checked my phone for the time. It was later than I'd realized—closer to evening.

Ty walked over and flopped next to me on the couch, and leaned their head on my shoulder. With anyone else, it might be weird, a little too close, but Ty made it comfortable. There was a certain easiness to them that made you want to tell them all of your secrets and worries.

"They sound good," they said, soft enough that I didn't think anyone else could hear. They raised a hand to brush their hair back from their eyes. Bracelets sparkled on their wrist, clinking softly together, a cascade of color against their skin.

I held still so I wouldn't jostle them. "They sound like they can't agree on anything."

The band had paused again as we talked. Ava had flung up her hands, then dropped her sticks down on her snare. Bellamy and Tuck were arguing again, truly this time, about the same doubled chorus. It was mostly civil so far, but I wasn't sure how long that would last.

"It's too long if you double it. It drags." Bellamy's hands had started to fly, catching on the microphone cord. His voice was rising the tiniest bit too. There was a tension in his shoulders that told me he was getting ready to storm off.

Tuck knew Bellamy even better than I did, but he seemed too wrapped up in his own concerns at the moment to notice. He held his hand up. "But the bridge doesn't work, either. It sounds fucking weird. I don't want it like that." He leaned forward, poking his hand in the air to make his point.

I started to get up, not sure exactly what I'd do or say. Just knowing I could maybe handle this, that I was usually the person who stepped in when tensions were running high. But Micah, who'd been sitting with Ben at the soundboard, slipped out of his seat and into the other room before I could get off the couch. He didn't call to Bellamy, or gesture for him to calm down. He didn't need to. I'd seen him work his magic on Bellamy before, lots of times, and I still couldn't figure out how he did it. Bellamy caught his eye, and they held that gaze for a minute. And when Bellamy turned back to Tuck, he still looked angry, but steadier too.

I sighed and relaxed back against the couch. I felt . . . odd. I was glad Bellamy had Micah, and watching them together was like watching magic. Seeing how they fit, how they seemed to be able to communicate with gestures and glances. But it made me feel like I was adrift too. Taking care of Bellamy had been my job. And now someone else was doing it.

"They'll get it," Ty said, bringing me back to the present and the couch. "It takes a little bit." They gestured over at Danni. "I almost killed her today. Over a chord change, of all things."

I laughed. "I doubt that."

They raised their eyebrows at me. "Oh yeah? You underestimating me?" Their tone was joking, but it had an edge of seriousness in it too.

I shook my head. "Never."

I glanced back at the other side of the divided room. Bellamy and Tuck seemed to have settled down a little, and Ava was leaning forward across her snare drum, listening to them. The microphone was picking up the quiet click of her sticks where she was rattling them against her knee. Micah had come back out and sat down, and he had his phone out. He was playing a game or something, totally calm, like he hadn't just averted a crisis. Not that Bellamy was the type to throw a fit over anything. But he'd storm out, and Tuck would get angry, and then the next few hours would be wasted.

It looked like they weren't going to be playing anything for at least a few minutes. I'd already heard them play a thousand versions of this song, anyway. I excused myself from Ty and Danni and went to find the restroom. When I came out, instead of going back to the studio room Escaping Indigo was in, I wound my way through the narrow halls, until I came out at the door that opened onto the wide driveway. I stepped out, careful not to let the door latch behind me.

I leaned back against the side of the building. It was rough rock, unfinished, like someone had hacked this side of the studio out of the hill. It was warm, though, and I closed my eyes and let the sun seep into me through my T-shirt. The studio was fascinating, but I didn't quite know how I felt about being underground, without any windows, for so long.

There was a slight scuffling noise from the other side of the building.

"Don't let the door close!" Nicky said as he came around the corner.

"I didn't." I pointed at the rock that was wedged between the door and the frame. "I didn't know you were out here."

He sighed and came to stand next to me. He held up his hand, showing me the cigarette he had tucked between two fingers. "Bad habit." He glanced sideways at me. "You want one?"

I shook my head, ready to say no. I'd stopped smoking a few months ago, but the habit of the short, private moments the cigarettes had provided was almost harder to break than the nicotine addiction. I'd been really good, though. I'd chewed gum and told myself I had willpower, and I'd done the stupid patch thing for a while. Mostly it had worked. But Nick's cigarette smelled nice, peppery and green. And I liked the way he was holding it, so casual and comfortable.

"Can I just . . .?" I reached out.

He nodded and handed it over without a pause. I put it to my lips and took a drag. The paper was dry and warm, and I couldn't help thinking, like a teenager sipping out of their crush's soda can, that his lips had been right there. A smoky, secondhand kiss.

I handed the cigarette back. I figured one of us would make an excuse and go in then, but neither of us moved. Nick took a drag, and I watched him. Maybe it was weird, to stare at him while he smoked. But he was standing so close. And he looked so good when he did it.

He had tattoos all the way up his right arm. I remembered seeing those tattoos shifting with his movements, the colors muted by darkness. The feel of the skin when I ran my hand over it, slightly raised, velvety where the ink was. I gestured at his wrist.

"Did you get a new one?"

He turned his wrist over to stare at it, like he'd forgotten himself that it was there. I probably shouldn't have noticed. But I'd liked looking at his tattoos, and I didn't remember the blue bird.

He smiled. "Yeah. Do you like it?"

I nodded. It was pretty. A delicate thing against a well-muscled arm. Incongruous and all the more beautiful because of that.

There was a peach next to it, inked in pale colors and a thin outline. I remembered that one. I remembered running my thumb over it while he slept, and telling myself I'd ask him about it. I'd forgotten the next morning, though, and then he'd been headed off with his band, and I'd never gotten the chance.

I reached out and touched it now, featherlight. "I meant to ask you about this. Is it for your band?" When he nodded, I asked, "Where did you get that name, anyway?"

He laughed. He drew his arm away too. It was a subtle movement, so it wasn't like he was yanking away from my touch. But that's almost what it felt like.

"It was a typo. Some friend of a friend on Facebook. Her cat died, and in the comments on the post, someone had written 'rest in peach.'" He laughed softly, the sound slightly melancholy, and I smiled back at him. "It was like this bit of ridiculousness." He waved his hand through the air. "This super-sad post, and this person's trying to be so serious, but I'm cracking up imagining this cat resting in peach." He glanced at me, looking mischievous and a bit guilty.

Then he sighed and leaned against the wall, closing his eyes, his head tipped back so his throat looked long. "But I thought, 'Isn't it awesome that in this grief, something funny happens too? Something funny actually comes out of it.'" He blinked open his eyes and stared straight ahead, but I didn't think he was actually seeing anything. "Like, life goes on, you know? And sadness and laughter can exist at the same time." He shrugged. "So when we were trying to come up with a band name, I said it as a joke. But it stuck. And now I have a peach tattooed on my arm." He flipped his hand over to see it, like he couldn't quite remember what it looked like. "Every time I see it, I think of that."

I nodded. I didn't know what to say. I liked the story. I liked that their name had some meaning, at least to Nick. But what he'd said about laughter and grief, and life going on, hit me in the pit of my stomach, and for a moment, I couldn't speak. I couldn't think past the idea.

He dropped the last of the cigarette and stubbed it out under the toe of his sneaker. Then he turned to face me. "Look, Quinn. When I said I thought maybe I'd hear from you . . . I'm sorry. I didn't mean to put you on the spot. That wasn't what . . ."

"You wouldn't have said it if you didn't want me to reply to it," I said, before I could think better of it, or stop myself. Or both.

He blinked, like he was surprised.

"Sorry," I said quickly. "Sorry, sorry. That, uh. That didn't come out right."

For a second, his face was completely blank. Then he laughed. "You're right. I *did* want to know why you never wanted to hook up with me again. But I truly didn't mean to ask you like that. And it's in the past, right?" He seemed hopeful, like I'd agree with that and let the subject drop. "I didn't want to start some awkward, accusatory thing. I want . . . We're all here and it should be fun. Not about stuff that happened before."

I nodded. But apparently I wasn't done running my mouth. "I did want to. Hook up with you again." I swallowed. My throat was dry all of a sudden. "See you again. I did."

He shrugged, but the movement was tight and quick. "I called. You didn't call back. So."

"Yeah." I'd thought, before, that if it was the two of us alone, maybe I'd be able to tell him. Explain, although it wasn't really any kind of explanation. Tell him about Eric and everything that had happened and how messed up I'd been afterward. How seeing anyone hadn't really been an option. But I couldn't make myself. The words were right there, but there was no way they were coming out of my mouth. I didn't know how Micah did it. He . . . blurted it out to people. Like he was getting it over with before it could do more damage. Like he was putting it out there for everyone to see, so they'd know exactly what hurt him the most. That scared me. It was terrifying. I didn't want anyone to know how much pain I was in. Even though I'd had a year to get used to the idea that my brother was dead.

"I had . . . I couldn't," I said instead.

For a second, Nick went still, and I thought he might press it, ask for more of an answer. He deserved it. We'd only been together for those few weeks, had only had sex the once. But it had been . . . more than a one-night thing. We'd been friends, or on the way to being friends. He could have demanded an explanation, and he would have had every right.

He didn't, though. He only nodded and glanced away. The movement wasn't as uncomfortable as the shrug had been, but I could see all the hurt and anger in it, all the things he was trying to hide from me. The stress and the uncertainty under his skin.

"I'm sorry," I said again, because I didn't like that expression on him. And I definitely didn't want to be the one causing it. "It wasn't you. It wasn't anything like that. Anything between the two of us."

One corner of his mouth lifted up into a smile. "It really is fine."

Sometimes, when I let my mind wander—and it wandered its inevitable way to Nicky, because he was a burr in my brain—I thought about what it would have been like if I had answered those calls. Or tried to get in touch. Back then, I would have had to tell him what was going on. There wouldn't have been any way to hide it. I'd only been able to keep it from Bellamy and Tuck and Ava because we were on break at the time—we'd finished the tour not long before that, we were all going our separate ways for rest and family time, and then they went into the studio to record. It was six months before I had to spend any length of time with them. And I'd had a perfect excuse for avoiding them for all that time—I'd told them I was traveling to see family. In a way, I had. We'd put Eric in the family plot, which was in a graveyard in Nevada. I figured Eric would probably laugh about that. He'd hated going to Nevada for those family trips.

But if I'd returned Nick's calls, if I'd seen him, he'd have known. He'd have known about everything I was dealing with, and he'd have seen how much . . . pain and confusion and anger I was caught in. He probably would have been supportive. Kind. He was the type of person who could gather you in and make you feel held, just by putting his arm around your shoulders. He would have wanted to hold me together as best he could. Might have wanted to be there for me, as a friend if nothing else. I could never have asked that of him, when whatever was between us was so new and fragile. Letting it fade away was the better option.

I cleared my throat. "I'm still sorry about it. It was a shitty thing to do."

He nodded. "Thanks."

I didn't know what else to say after that. I thought it would get weird and tense, and I'd have to make an excuse to get away. But it wasn't. It wasn't exactly comfortable, either. We really didn't know each other now, after more than a year had passed since the last time we'd been together, the last time we'd spoken. Nicky had always been easy to be with, though. It was the first thing that had drawn me to him. He made things simple. He made you want to stand beside him and soak up some sun. So I did.

# chapter three

X

**e**scaping Indigo started to get into the swing of recording over the next day or two. They split their day into two parts: one to write new stuff and straighten out the songs they did have, and another to record. Sometimes they did the writing in the morning, sometimes in the afternoon and evening. It depended, mostly, on how they were feeling.

There wasn't a lot for me and Micah to do. We could sit there and listen and say we liked something, or liked this other something better, but that was pretty much it. When they were writing, the band got lost in each other, this relationship that was as intense and inclusive as any close friendship or love affair. Different, of course. But there was something that happened between the three of them when they were making music that no one else could touch or come into. As if the music wrapped around them and held everyone else out.

Micah was used to being a musician's partner. He'd done it for years for Eric, for all that they'd been friends and not lovers. I remembered coming into the apartment the two of them had shared and seeing them sitting side by side on the couch, Micah with his eyes on a book, Eric holding his guitar and picking out chords. It hadn't looked like Micah was paying any attention, but if Eric paused and asked him something, he not only had a response, but thoughtful things to say about whatever music Eric was making. Micah was doing the same thing now, except he'd exchanged the book for a sketchpad and a pencil. When Escaping Indigo went into their world, he went into his, and he only came out if one of them needed him.

I couldn't quite do that. As much as I loved the band and knew they wanted my opinions, and took what I said seriously, I always thought of myself as very slightly separate. I worked for them. I took care of them. And they made the music. That was something I didn't do, had never done.

On the third day of recording, I was sitting next to Ben at the soundboard, watching him push buttons up and down, adjusting sounds and bringing vocals to the front, and generally doing a bunch of stuff I had no clue about. I'd been watching him do it for days, but I didn't think I'd ever really understand.

Bellamy was on his other side, and they were talking in half sentences about levels and measures. I'd wondered whether Bellamy would be okay as a producer—some bands liked to produce their own stuff, and others wanted someone to help them. But somewhere along the line, Bellamy had picked up a lot, and he seemed to know what he was doing. And Ben seemed happy to fill in the gaps too.

I glanced through the window in front of us to the main recording room. Ava was tapping away at her snare, very softly, while she talked to Tuck. She caught my eye and waved, but she was involved in her conversation. I waved back and turned to Bellamy and Ben again.

I had to clear my throat to get their attention. On my other side, Micah stifled a laugh.

"Would it be okay if I wandered around the studio?" I asked Ben when he finally focused on me.

He pinched his eyebrows together and pushed his glasses up his nose. "Of course. Why wouldn't it be?"

I shrugged, surprised. "'Cause it's your house?" I didn't mention that he might be justifiably worried about all the expensive equipment he had around too.

He laughed, but it wasn't an unkind sound. "Knock yourself out. I don't know how interesting it'll be. They're empty rooms, mostly."

Behind him, Bellamy was peering over his shoulder at me. "I can go with you, later, when we're done here." I heard Micah take a breath, as if he was going to offer the same thing.

I shook my head and stood up. "That'd be cool. But I'm fine on my own for right now."

Bellamy cocked his head, studying me, but then he nodded.

"There's a couple rooms in the back with couches and stuff, if you want to chill," Ben said. He was already turning back to the board and Bellamy and their conversation.

I nodded, but he wasn't paying attention to me anymore. I wondered if Ben was choosy about what bands got to record here, and that was why he didn't care if I poked around the place he lived. I wondered if he only picked people he liked, or thought he'd like. He was certainly well known and sought after enough to do that.

Micah raised his eyebrows at me, but I just smiled back at him and lifted my hand in a wave before I made my way to the door.

There were *a lot* of rooms down here—a warren of big and small spaces, all for different purposes. Mostly storage—musicians brought their own gear, and tended to stick with it, but if someone needed a cymbal that was slightly sandier in sound, or an effect pedal that did this particular weird thing, or that perfect guitar that they wouldn't get to use anywhere else, Ben probably had it. There were several different rooms to record in too. Small glassed-in rooms for vocals—some wood paneled and warm, with thick, dark red carpets and lamps set on tables. Other were rougher, more raw, the walls close and painted a dark gray, so it seemed like they were built right into the rock of the hill. They were all still and silent now, microphones and flimsy stools left seemingly abandoned.

There were bigger rooms too. Medium-sized rooms for drums, so cymbals wouldn't bleed into guitar sounds. Rooms that faced one of the soundboards—most of the rooms faced one soundboard or another—rooms with huge glass walls, black in the darkness, until I flicked on a light. Rooms with double walls to make the sound quality better, richer. One room with an entire second room built underneath it, and a gap all the way around the floor, so the air space was doubled.

I wandered into one empty room and flicked on the light switch, only to realize this room was attached to the one Escaping Indigo was working in. Somehow I'd walked in a circle and hadn't realized it. Everyone turned to stare at me, and Ava waved cheerfully. It was almost a shock—I'd been so lost in the space and the muffled sound of distant music that I forgot for a minute that anyone else was down here with me. I waved back, shut the light off again, and moved on.

After that, I went on in the dark without turning any more lights on. I wanted to explore by myself. I caught glimpses of the band as they sat around and worked or talked. Sometimes I saw them through two or three reflecting glass walls, so the image was all bouncy and skewed. But unless they stared into the darkness, they didn't seem able to see me at all.

I was still uncomfortable with being underground, even though it was technically really a huge basement. Some of the rooms I explored were actually above ground, in what had once been the garage. But there weren't any windows to the outside—regular windows and recording music weren't a good mix—and it was like being buried, sometimes. Trapped. Locked away in muffling walls and rock that had heard hundreds and hundreds of songs, hundreds of conversations and arguments and shared jokes between band members. That had seen history being made, and had probably seen bands fail and fall apart too. Thinking of it in that way made it more immersive than frightening, although it was still overwhelming in a lot of ways.

Every now and then I escaped upstairs, to the bright kitchen, or to the bedroom I was sharing with Tuck, with its many windows looking out onto green lawn, or out the back door, to stand on cracked pavement and breathe in fresh air. And when I was standing in the sunlight, I'd wonder why I was letting my mind go down those paths, about music and history. I wondered what it was about this place, this process, that was making me think about things I'd never really considered before. Or about things I'd been able to push down for most of a year. Things I'd thought I was finally coming to terms with, able to live with.

I didn't have an answer. When it felt like too much heaviness, I'd go back to the band instead, and surrounded myself with their music and laughter. Then I could remind myself that everything was normal, even when it felt, sometimes, as if something important had clicked out of place.

On one of my excursions the fourth day we were there, I wandered into the other half of the studio, near where Rest in Peach was recording. As it was with the rooms where Escaping Indigo was playing, there were several rooms here, loosely surrounding the room with the soundboard. The vocals booth was ready for use, the lamps on, creating a soft, almost cozy glow. Two walls of the booth were glass, and from the hallway, I could see through, into the room beyond, where Rest in Peach was in the middle of a song. The sound was slightly muffled—if I'd been standing by the mixing board, it would be crystal clear. But I could still hear it, and it was enough to make me think it was going to be an amazing album, loud and sweet and raw and tender, like all of their music. A strange mix, Ty liked to call it, and that was accurate.

I felt a little odd, standing here, almost spying on them while they played. But this was a recording studio. Standing and listening to music was what this space was built for. Still, I didn't want to intrude or be distracting. I leaned back against the wall, tucking myself away in the shadows, and listened.

Rest in Peach's music was different than Escaping Indigo's. No one could say that what Tuck, Bellamy, and Ava wrote was straightforward, but it was more reliably rock based, more . . . familiar in its feel. Which was effective, because by the time you picked up on the lyrics, or all the slight intricacies and oddities in the sound and the melody and the way the band played, you were already hooked. But Rest in Peach didn't care about being familiar in any way. They were bold and aggressive, and at the same time, delicate and beautiful in their sounds. And it worked just as well to draw listeners in.

I liked them because of how different they sounded, how refreshing their songs were. And I liked what Ty sang about—being in love, or in lust, feeling left out, feeling like you were loved by your friends, being the person who was a little on the outside, being accepted. Dichotomous and opposing themes in the same album, sometimes in the same song.

I hadn't closed my eyes, but when the song ended, it seemed like I was falling back down to earth, coming out of the music in a way, and landing here, in a dim hallway. And when I blinked and looked up, Nicky was staring into my eyes.

He was watching me. Staring right at me, like he had the very first day. No hiding it, no glancing away to make it seem like he wasn't. He didn't seem to care if I knew that was what he was doing. But it wasn't aggressive or possessive or anything. It was . . . like he was curious. Like he was taking me in and trying to figure me out from a distance.

My first instinct was to look down myself. Pretend this wasn't happening. I'd gotten involved with Nick before, and it had been . . . wonderful. But it had been a fantasy, and it wasn't ever meant to last.

But I didn't turn away. I couldn't. His face was so open. His whole body was turned toward me—the angle of the drums made that happen, but there was something in the set of his shoulders and the twist of his waist that almost made it like he was holding himself open for me. For my stare.

I pulled in a harsh breath. This was . . . intense. Intense and not what I'd expected, definitely not what I'd been prepared for when I walked down this hallway. Nick was all sweaty and slightly out of breath, like that first day, and he was hot. There was absolutely no denying that. He was incredibly . . . hot. I wanted him. Watching him like this, our gazes connected, made me remember all the ways we'd connected in the past—with our bodies, by sharing a joke, by catching that private smile he had, just for me, out of the corner of my eye.

But mostly, I was obsessed with the way it felt to have his eyes and his attention on me. Solely on me. That focus, like I could feel it on my skin. I remembered that from when we'd toured together. The way I'd glance up from setting up Ava's kit or laying out cords and find him watching me from the other side of the stage. Back then, he'd always blushed and turned away. Now he didn't. Now, he was bold, but I wasn't offended by it. I liked the sensation too much. It was addictive and I wanted more of it.

Nicky glanced to the side. Elliot was talking to him, drawing him into a conversation. I couldn't make out any words. I started to turn, to walk back the way I'd come. Now that the stare was broken and I was remembering where I was, who we all were and what we were here for, I felt silly. That couldn't possibly have been as intimate a moment as I'd imagined. But Nicky put his sticks down on his snare, balancing them carefully against the rim, and stood up. He gestured out to the hall—not to me, I was pretty sure, but that direction in general. Ty and Elliot nodded, and Danni turned away from her keyboard.

Then Nicky was coming out of the studio door before I could disappear back to our own studio, or outside, or upstairs, or anywhere that would take me away from this . . . whatever this was.

"Hey."

"We should stop meeting like this," I blurted, and it was a joke, but I was almost half serious too.

Nick grinned at me. "Maybe. But I kind of like it."

I turned to face him, because I was an adult, a grown man, and there was no way I was running and hiding from a scary social situation. I gestured toward the recording room. "It sounded really good, back there. Really . . ." Fuck, I was so bad with words. I never knew how to describe anything so it made sense.

Nick smiled at me, though. "Thanks. We're happy with it, so far." His voice was soft, almost like he didn't want to say it too loudly and jinx anything. But there was a quiet confidence behind his words too. "We want to still sound like us, you know? But . . . new."

I nodded. It was a simple way to put something that wasn't simple at all. And doing that was treading on a fine line.

Nicky raised a hand and rubbed it over the back of his neck, suddenly awkward. Or more awkward, now that we didn't have a ready conversation topic. Then he sighed sharply, as if he'd decided something, and gestured down the hall toward the stairs leading up to the house. "I'm going to grab some lunch. Want to come?"

I hesitated, but then I nodded. There wasn't any reason not to. Nick and I had mutually agreed to leave the past in the past, and I wanted things to be easy between us again. We'd all—Escaping Indigo and Rest in Peach—gone out to dinner last night. It had been simple and fun, like when we'd been on tour together. Friends hanging out. This wouldn't be any different. Just smaller scale.

Nicky led me up the stairs, then around to the back door out of the studio. We circled the house and came out on the sidewalk. Nick stopped and turned back to look at the place. From here, it seemed like nothing more than a big house with a slightly oddly shaped garage. Aside from the two large trailers and abundance of cars in the driveway, there was hardly anything to distinguish it from any other house on the block. No music leaked out from the studio. It was clean and quiet and calm from here. Not the raucous, rowdy party atmosphere I might have assumed of a rock music mecca. No people spilling half-clothed out of doorways. No one sleeping on the lawn. No wailing guitars, screeching into the still air of the neighborhood.

I'd bet it had seen some things, though.

"I probably drove by it when I was a kid." Nick turned back to me. He shaded his eyes, smiling faintly. He looked almost a bit nervous, and as much as I didn't want him to be anxious to be with me, it made me feel better to see it. Like all the emotions tumbling through me might be normal.

"Did you live far from here?"

He shook his head and started walking. "No, not far. I don't know why I would have come down this street, I guess. But if I had—if I did—I wouldn't have realized what was there."

"Do you like it?" It was so bright out. Half of me wished I'd brought a pair of sunglasses to block all the sunlight bouncing off the pavement, flickering up in waves of heat. But the other half was glad I hadn't. I had to squint to see Nicky, so I kept my eyes on the ground in front of me instead, and it made it easier to talk to him. To walk beside him.

"Oh, yeah," he answered like it was obvious. "It's the dream, right?" He laughed, and it sounded sharp and hard, as if there was some reason he shouldn't be allowed to admit that. To admit he'd had a dream, and had done what he could to make it reality. "I mean . . ." He waved his hand through the air. "I didn't honestly ever think this would happen. Ty and Danni and Elliot . . . they never believed anything else. They wanted it and they were going to do whatever it took to make it happen. Me . . . I wanted it. I wanted it so much. More than anything. But I didn't think it would actually happen. I thought it was a fantasy."

I was smiling now. He said it all so simply, as if it was a stream of consciousness. Like the details of his life, of how he'd gotten where he was, had fallen from the sky. Like they weren't that important. But there was this thread of something close to awe in his voice. As if he knew exactly how lucky he was.

I didn't think it was all luck, though.

"But you did make it happen," I said.

He nodded and glanced back at me. He was walking slightly ahead of me. I was okay with that. Usually, I tended to care very little about how people looked. But Nick was different. He was striking and lean, and he walked with an easy confidence that put a swing in his hips. I liked the way his hips moved a lot. I liked that confidence more.

"Yeah, we did. And now we're recording. It gets me every time. As close as we come to immortality, you know? Making it permanent. Like putting it down on paper." He laughed again, lighter this time. "Except not really like that."

"I know what you mean, I think." Eric and Micah had never recorded like this, with a producer and techs in a fancy studio. But they'd paid for studio time at a place near our house, and they'd recorded stuff in the garage by themselves. I had a lot of those recordings, and sometimes, when I was feeling either particularly strong or particularly lonely, I took them out and listened to them. Listened to my brother's voice coming through headphones, right into my heart. Listened to the sound of his hands sliding on guitar strings. Listened to the things he had written, the things he had created. The things he had left behind.

It *was* immortality, in a way. It was like . . . no matter what, he'd brought something true and purely him into the world, and it was still here, would still be here, with any luck, for years and years. For as long as it was saved. After I was gone. After Micah was. There might still be that music.

"Do you really think so?" I asked. We'd been walking along, neither of us speaking, while I turned those thoughts over in my head. We were passing under an orange tree that hung over the sidewalk. It was in bloom, and when I stopped, I could smell the scent of the flowers, thick and sticky sweet around me. "About making music being like some type of immortality?"

Nick stopped too, and turned around to face me. His expression had gone serious and I wondered how my voice sounded, to make him look like that. But I was having . . . a thing, a thought, something was going on in my mind and my heart, and I wasn't sure I was entirely in control of what came out of my mouth.

He nodded, slowly. "Yeah. I really do. Quinn, are you okay?"

I didn't know why, there, under the shade from the orange tree, with the heat from the sidewalk pooling up around us, the smell of exhaust and white petals, I could say what I hadn't been able to before. What I'd struggled so hard with yesterday, and all the days prior. Maybe it was simply the right moment now. Here. Maybe I couldn't hold it in one second longer.

"My brother died."

My focus snapped away from whatever thoughts of Eric and whatever ideas about music I'd been having, and into myself, as if saying the words had released some tension. I came back down in time to see Nick's face go through a range of emotions. Shock and sadness and horror and fear and confusion and pity. He settled back on sadness, and I was relieved. If he'd gone with pity, I wouldn't have been able to stand it. I'd had enough of that to last a lifetime.

"When?" he asked, and it was another surprise, a good one—he didn't say he was sorry or offer some platitude. He went for the facts first. I liked that, especially coming from him. I already knew he was kind. It was good to know he was logical too.

"Right after the tour when you and I met. I went home, everything was fine. Or I thought it was fine. And then he overdosed and he was dead."

Nick paled, maybe at how bluntly I'd put it, but I kept talking, determined not to give him a chance to say anything until I'd gotten this all out. I'd started—I might as well finish it.

"It was an accident. Just . . . an accident." I swallowed. "That's why I didn't return your calls. Why I didn't ever reach out. I didn't know how to say it. I didn't know . . ." The air in front of me shimmered, and I swayed. I'd forgotten what it was like, to say all of that out loud. Like I was making it more real, cementing the truth of it, by putting it into words.

Nick took a step forward, so he was nearly in my personal space. Not quite. But close enough I imagined I could feel the warmth of him, despite the hot Los Angeles breeze between us. I liked it, even if it was an illusion. "I had no idea," he said.

I smiled at him. It was probably lopsided and wrong, because I wasn't in a smiling mood at all. But it had been a relief to tell him.

That was a surprise. "I know. I didn't want you to. I figured you'd have wanted . . . to do something for me."

He nodded and frowned. "I would have, yeah."

"But we didn't know each other well enough," I replied, trying to explain.

"If you mean you fucking me silly didn't equal us knowing each other, I'm gonna have to beg to differ."

"That was—"

He held up a hand before I could finish. "Say it was 'just sex,' and I'll walk away right now."

I sighed, and slumped. "No. It . . . wasn't." It was good to say that. To get it out there. I hadn't been sure, really, whether it had only been me who'd felt that, at the time. Like whatever small thing we'd started had been something important enough, something it seemed like we could build on it. "But we really *didn't* know each other well. Not in any other way. We were . . . friends, maybe? And I didn't think you needed . . . I didn't want to get you involved. I wasn't your responsibility."

He didn't pull back, but it seemed like he stepped away somehow anyway. "I get it."

"It wasn't personal, Nicky. I didn't do it to hurt you. I wanted to . . . I didn't know what I was doing. For a long time." I pushed my hair back with my fingers. It was sticky with sweat at my temples. "I still don't."

He nodded. "I do get it," he said, softer this time.

His voice was so gentle. At some point, he'd touched his fingertips to my elbow, as if he was anchoring me, or anchoring himself, and he hadn't let go. And for some reason, the gentleness, the tenderness in the gesture and the words, made me think I might cry.

I hadn't cried in . . . I couldn't remember how long. Not when Eric died. Not when we had his funeral. Micah had cried. I'd heard him, in his apartment, when he forgot to close the windows. I'd stood outside, a floor down, and listened to the sound of his grief pour out. But I hadn't let mine. There had been too much to do, too much to take care of. I'd had to be steady for my mom, for Micah. I'd had to be strong so the band wouldn't know. I had already fucked up the most important job I'd had—taking care of Eric. Being there for him. I wasn't going to fuck up any more, if I could help it. The band would have seen me differently, especially in those first months. Tuck would have tried to make me take time off. I couldn't have handled that, not then. I needed them, the band and my role with them, to be normal. Crying in front of them would have ruined that.

But there was something about Nicky, some closeness he made me feel, that put me right on the edge.

"I'd like to hug you, but I think I might break if I do," he said, and it was so perfect and so what I was feeling that I laughed out loud. The laugh was watery and strained but it was honest, and it was good.

"Sorry." I took a deep breath, trying to center myself. "Sorry. I really didn't mean to blurt all that out. Lay it on you like that."

He shook his head. His hand was still on my elbow, the touch light against my skin. I hoped he wouldn't move. "Probably the best way to do it, really. Like taking off a Band-Aid."

I told myself I was okay. This was fine. I straightened my spine and met Nick's eyes. "Do you want to go get that lunch?"

"Yeah, but . . . in a minute." He slipped his hand down my arm and wrapped his fingers around mine, our palms pressed tight together. Then he pulled me over to a patch of grass. "Sit with me for a second."

The grass was shaded by a different tree, and the cool, deep green of it *was* tempting. But I was pretty sure it was private property. "I think this is someone's lawn."

He waved his free hand through the air. "It's fine. It's only for a minute. We're not going to do anything but sit."

He was so eager and earnest about it, I did as he'd asked and sat beside him. The grass was tucked in front of and between two houses, ending at the sidewalk. If I stretched my legs out, my heels hit pavement. There was a low, decorative stone wall behind us, and it shielded us. We were in plain sight, but I didn't think we were actually on display if anyone glanced out their window.

Nick still had my hand in his. He twisted his fingers through mine. "I just . . . wanted to talk to you for a second. And I didn't want to do it at the restaurant or whatever."

I started to shake my head. This was some big emotional thing for me to have said, yeah. But this was enough. I didn't want to talk about it anymore. Everything in me rebelled at the idea.

He must have seen the expression on my face, because he smiled. Still gentle, but a little bit teasing too. "Don't worry. I get it. I'm not gonna go all Dr. Phil on you." He squeezed my hand. I wondered if he was conscious of how connected we were there. How electric it was to be skin to skin. Or if he was as open and tactile with everyone. I couldn't remember. I remembered the ways he'd touched me when we'd worked together, the brushes of fingers, or shoulders against shoulders. I'd tried to memorize each one. But that had been flirting, and I hadn't noticed if he was that way with anyone else.

"Thought you might want a minute before we walked into a public place too," he added.

I nodded. That was thoughtful. And probably true, although I didn't really want to admit to it.

"How old was he?" Nick asked softly.

"Twenty-four."

His thumb brushed over the inside of my wrist. "He was a musician? That's why you asked about . . . music being like immortality?"

"Yeah." I swallowed and took a deep breath. I couldn't look at him while I talked about Eric. "He . . . It was like he lived in the music, you know? One of those people who almost exists somewhere outside of everything real? He was good." I dropped my gaze to our hands, lying in the grass. "He was really good."

Nick was quiet for a long time. I wondered if maybe we'd get up in a minute, and that would be it. We'd let the whole thing go. I started to hope for it. It wouldn't solve anything, but it would be the easiest thing—I'd found that out, over the last year. If I wanted to keep living, keep moving—and I did—I had to make a conscious effort not to think about Eric until I was prepared for it. Maybe someday it would get easier, and I'd be able to think about him without this terrible mess of sadness and guilt, but I couldn't yet.

Most days, my strategy worked just fine. I wasn't getting over my brother's death. I was learning to live with it, though.

Nick untangled our hands and dropped his in his lap.

"I have a son," he said. "He's two."

I blinked. Of all the things I might have guessed he'd say in this particular moment, that wasn't anywhere on the list. It was so out of left field it was baffling.

"What?" It definitely wasn't the best thing to say, but I honestly didn't think I could come up with anything else.

He glanced up at me, then away. "I didn't tell you before because . . . It's not like I don't want to talk about him." He gave me an embarrassed smile. "It's just that I'm . . . protective? And I didn't know where we stood, me and you. I would have . . . I would have told you, if we got together again. I would have wanted to."

I nodded, trying to absorb that. I wasn't angry he hadn't told me. It made sense. But I was trying to sort what I thought I knew about Nick, and what I obviously didn't, together.

"How did . . ." I waved my hand, trying to voice my question without actually saying it. "You and his mother . . . are you . . .?" I wasn't sure why I was asking. Just that I wanted to know.

He shook his head. "His mother and I had hooked up for . . . god, maybe a few days? Got careless. We never got back together or anything. It's better this way. We can . . . work as a team with him, in a way."

I didn't have the first idea how to process that, how to answer it. What to say. Kids were a completely foreign concept to me. I hadn't ever considered them myself, except in the most abstract ways. It always made me feel so old when one of my friends had one. Made me realize how much we'd grown. Made me feel like my reality and their reality were completely out of skew.

Nicky had plucked up a blade of grass, and he was twisting it around and around his finger.

"Do you get to see him?" I asked, finally.

He looked up at me and nodded, and relaxed slightly. "Yeah. Every weekend, for now. And holidays and stuff. I was going to switch my weekend for a weekday instead, while we're recording, but I wanted to show him the studio. Ben said it's fine."

"Oh."

"You could meet him, when he's here. If you want. I'd like that."

I nodded. "Okay."

He raised his hands, and the grass fluttered to the ground. He turned them palm up, as if in supplication. But then he just stared down at them. He had such long fingers. I'd heard that was something that benefited guitar players and keyboardists. I remembered Eric staring at his hands and trying to figure out how to get them to make the complicated shapes he needed for the chords. I wasn't sure if it was useful at all for a drummer. I didn't really know anything about any of that. I could tune a guitar with one of those little pedals that lit up when you hit the right spot. But that was about as musical as I got.

"What's his name?" I asked. I was only curious, but Nicky turned to me and grinned, and I knew it had been the right thing to say.

"Josh. Joshua." He'd dropped his hands, and he seemed a little adrift without anything to focus on. I wished he hadn't let go of my hand. It had been easier, somehow, to talk to him when we were connected. "It's so weird. All that time. I never thought about having kids. But now it's like I can't imagine my life without him in it, you know?"

I nodded. I understood that backward and forward—maybe more backward, because it was more, for me, about figuring out how my life worked with this giant hole where Eric had been. But I did understand it, on so many levels, and it was *still* a mystery how it worked. I didn't know how to say any of that to Nicky, though.

"I'm sorry," he continued. "You were telling me about your brother and I went and said something about myself."

He blinked at me. His face was always so open. I'd met a lot of musicians, and most of them had this . . . hardness to them. Like they'd been knocked around by life. Like the path to the stage had been incredibly difficult and it had scarred them in some way. And I figured Nicky had felt that. I knew he wasn't naïve to it. But he didn't have that haunted look in the back of his eyes. He didn't secret pieces of himself away, to keep when the world got to be a little too much. He was all right there, right up front.

"I . . . wanted to give you something in return," he said, softer. "Something about myself."

I brushed my fingers over his knee. He was wearing comfortable shorts, to drum in, so I grazed fabric, then bare skin, the hair of his leg. It was the slightest touch, but it seemed intimate, weighty. I shouldn't have done it, probably. I just couldn't stop myself.

"You didn't have to do that."

He shrugged. I wondered if he'd felt that electric zing when I touched him too. Wondered if it had run through him like a current, the same way it had for me. Wondered if he was maybe better than me at pretending it hadn't happened. "You'd have known, anyway, when I have him this weekend."

I nodded. That was true. It didn't feel like that, though. It felt like he'd given me something special, by telling me here and now. Like I'd opened something up for him and he'd done his best to return the favor. "Thank you."

Nick nodded once, and stood up. He brushed his hands briskly over his backside, dislodging any stray pieces of grass. Then he held out his hand to me, and I let him pull me up beside him.

"I know you don't want to talk about it," he said as we started walking down the sidewalk again. He glanced at me, and our eyes met for a second before we both looked away. "And that's fine. But if you ever do, I'm good for that. Just . . . so you know."

"Thanks." I meant it. It made me uncomfortable. Horribly uncomfortable. It made me want to roll my shoulders in, hunch over myself, make my large frame as small as I could. But it made me warm inside, too, to know he would allow me that, either way.

He didn't push it, didn't make me agree to talk, or to acknowledge it much at all, and I was grateful. We carried on with our lunch plans, like we hadn't made that detour for awkward conversations. He took me to a burger place a few streets over. We sat inside, in the cool air-conditioning, and drank milk shakes and ate French fries that we dipped into a puddle of ketchup on a wrapper between us on the table. We talked about music, and the places we'd been since the last time we'd seen each other, and Nicky showed me pictures of his son. And it was easy.

When we got back to the studio, I was exhausted from all of it. From telling Nick about Eric, from simply . . . being with him and having all those emotions, untouched, in the air between us. But I was content in a strange way too. I went up to my room instead of going back down to see what Escaping Indigo was up to. I pulled out my laptop and played a game, to get some space to myself for a while. And for the first time since we'd gotten here, I felt more or less balanced, and safe, and okay.

# chapter four

X

t he next couple of days followed the same routine, more or less. I watched the band write and record, watched Ben doing all kinds of stuff with the board and its hundreds of switches, eavesdropped on conversations with Rest in Peach's producer. I explored the studio and all its back rooms. I looked at the pictures on the walls and tried to figure out how many had people in them I'd heard of, listened to. Admired. It was a lot of them. And in the evenings, we got together with Rest in Peach and went for dinner, or ordered in and ate standing around Ben's kitchen or scattered over his couches. Ty and Bellamy and Nick talked about past tours. Ava and Danni and Tuck and Elliot talked about what it had been like making music before they had access to real stages or recording studios like this, or a record label to back them. Micah and Ben and I hung out and listened, and joined in wherever, and I never felt for a second like we were left out or less than because we weren't actually members of either band. It was the opposite, for me at least—I was included, and I felt like even here, in this world that had always belonged more to my brother and my friends, I was at home.

It was fun, the perfect way to relax and take it easy after what was, for the bands, an enjoyable but also very fraught and tension-filled experience.

Nick and I didn't go for lunch again. The first day after we talked, I went out with Escaping Indigo and Micah, to the same place Nicky had taken me. The next day, Ben took me around the studio, telling me stories about the different rooms, how they'd been built, who'd played there, what songs had been born there. I'd never seen Ben quite so animated before. He pointed at pictures and told stories that no one else would have known, about recording mishaps and how bands acted together, how songs were created. We missed lunch altogether, and ended up poking through the refrigerator afterward.

The third day, I sat at the kitchen island and ate a sandwich while I talked to my mom on the phone. She missed me, she said, but I was halfway sure she really meant that she missed *Micah*, and she wanted to know when he was coming home. I worried a little bit about that— not because I was jealous, quite. It was good for her to have Micah to fuss over and baby, because I wasn't exactly an ideal candidate for that. But I figured Micah would eventually move in with Bellamy, away from my mom. I didn't let it worry me too much, because at this point, I knew Micah. And I knew he wouldn't forget about her, no matter where he went.

The fourth day, I went back to wandering. I'd been, at this point, through every open space in the studio. There wasn't anything left to explore. But the empty rooms kept drawing me back to them. Each one was so different. As if Ben had been experimenting as he constructed and decorated each one. Going for different sound qualities and atmospheres and comfort levels. And they were *quiet*. It was so strange to me that they had seen, over the years, such a riot, such a complete interplay, of combined sound. So many instruments and voices, take after take. And now they were silent, lying dormant. Waiting.

I liked listening to Escaping Indigo and Rest in Peach. I liked the evening part better, when we were all together and hanging out, and it was easy and fun, like being on tour, without the threat of having to drive all night looming over me. I liked the recording part too, though. It was interesting—on a technical level, and more than that, in how the band worked together to create their songs.

But there was something about what they were doing in those rooms, together, that was solely about *them*. Bellamy, Tuck, and Ava and no one else, no matter whether Ben was in the room, or Micah, or me. And I wasn't jealous—it was cool they had this talent, and I respected them for it more than I could say, but it wasn't actually anything I wanted for myself. But there was something about the way they tuned in to each other, focused on each other, became almost like one mind when they were writing and working on songs, that made me feel . . . lost. On the outside. Like I was a puzzle piece that didn't quite fit. It made me lonely in an abstract way. It was ridiculous to feel like this, but I couldn't help it.

And sometimes, when I was sitting on the back couch, getting lost in the music and the repetition of playing a piece over and over, I'd imagine Eric there. I would almost be able to picture him, standing where Bellamy was standing. His fingers on guitar strings, like Tuck's were. Him turning around to speak to Micah at the drum set.

But it wasn't Micah at the kit, it was Ava. And Eric would never be in this place, doing what Escaping Indigo was doing. It didn't make me as sad as I'd have imagined. Eric was gone, and I'd come to terms with that a long time ago. Grief couldn't stay sharp forever. It had to dull, become manageable, because human beings were designed to carry on. Whether I liked it or not, that was what I was doing. Most days, I was glad for it, because I didn't want to live with guilt and hurt eating at me every second. But when I thought about everything Eric could have had, what it would have been like if it *were* him and Micah here, now, it made me . . . nostalgic, in a way. It made me miss something that had never existed to begin with.

It was when that sensation started to overwhelm me that I got up and wandered. I brought my phone along with me, and idly scrolled through Twitter while I walked, peeking into dim rooms. I needed some time apart from the music and the band, apart from what they made me think about and remember.

Once, I found my way to the back of the studio, where there was one of the lounge-type rooms Ben had told me about. When I flicked the light on, it illuminated two overstuffed couches, worn from everyone who had flopped on them over the years, and a smallish table stereo system with a CD and record player. There were about a thousand albums, too, in both formats, tucked into shelves underneath.

A few pairs of headphones sat next to the stereo, so I plugged one in and started pulling out albums and putting them on. I skipped through some songs, played snippets of others. Other albums I hadn't listened to in years, and I wanted to hear the whole thing, dissolve in those sounds. There were things I'd never heard too. B-sides and live recordings, and bands I was only vaguely familiar with.

Bellamy found me there a couple of hours later. I'd completely lost track of time, and he must have been sent to find me.

"What's all this?"

I turned to stare at him over my shoulder. "Treasure."

He laughed and sat next to me. "Definitely." He started pulling out albums and handing them to me, and plugged another pair of headphones in so he could listen too.

It was silly—either of us could have brought up any of those songs on our phones in a second. But there was some sense of discovery, adventure, in pouring through the cases and sleeves, looking over artwork and liner notes. It was almost like when a song you loved came on the radio, and it was as if you'd had a flash of luck. Bellamy's excitement was infectious, and we spent the entire evening down there, until Tuck and Ty formed a second rescue party and came to get us for dinner.

I went back the next day, and when I heard the soft shuffle of footsteps on the carpet, I figured it was Bellamy again, or maybe Micah, come to find me because I'd been gone too long. But when I turned around, Nicky was standing in the doorway, his shoulder bumped up against the jamb. Watching me, his eyelids heavy.

I pulled my headphones off and turned fully to look at him. He didn't move, and he didn't look guilty at being caught staring, either.

I was sitting on the floor, and felt oddly vulnerable down here, with him standing above me. It wasn't a sensation I was used to. I wasn't tall, particularly, but I was big. Carrying amps and drums around for years will put some muscle on you, and my body had been built for that. People didn't intimidate me. And Nicky himself, while taller than me, was a beanpole, a wiry length of fine bone and tendons. I could have picked him up and thrown him over my shoulder, no problem, if that was a thing he was into. But from here, it was like he had power over me. Maybe it wasn't even that he was standing above me. Maybe it was the way he was watching me. The way I got caught up in his gaze.

He gestured toward the albums. "I see you found Ben's stash."

I nodded. I was careful about what I pulled out—they were all alphabetized, and I didn't want to mess them up too much. But there were still CD cases and pages of artwork and liner notes spread out around me. "It's . . . impressive."

He let go of the doorframe and crossed the room to plop down beside me. His fingers sifted through the albums I had out. He picked up one record with bright colors splashed across the front, and the name of the band written in a narrow font at the bottom.

"I remember this." He flipped it over to see the track listing on the back. "God, I haven't heard this in years."

"Put it on," I said, impulsively. I turned the volume down on the speakers and pulled my headphones out.

"Did you already listen, though? We can hear something different."

I shook my head. "It's a good album. I don't know why I haven't listened to it for so long."

He hesitated, watching me, then slipped the record out of its cover, and carefully opened the lid of the record player to set it on the turntable. I didn't know why Ben had this one in vinyl when it was a newer album, but I liked that he did. Not that I actually believed vinyl sounded better—maybe I was a heathen but I was pretty sure having added pops and scratches in a song did not enhance the music—but there was something about the ritual of it, the careful, gentle way you had to treat a record, that was soothing. Watching Nicky do it was beautiful, those long-fingered hands of his grazing the sides of the record, careful not to press down. The precise way he brushed dust from the record surface with the little pad for that purpose, the way he set the needle down. It was all so simple, but he made it a thing of grace.

The first notes of the album rose up between us. I leaned forward and adjusted the sound, loud enough that we could hear, but not so loud that it would bleed out of the room, or that we couldn't talk if we wanted to.

But Nick didn't seem particularly inclined to talk over it, and that was fine with me. It was a strange thing, music. It was always moving forward. Some people get stuck in a certain time period, only ever listen to music from the seventies, or the nineties. It was impossible to do that while hanging out with Escaping Indigo, though. They were constantly listening to new stuff, evolving with every new sound and innovation that came along, and adding their own, and I got caught up in that in the best ways. I was sure it was the same with Nick and Rest in Peach.

Which didn't mean I never listened to older stuff. But when there was so much to take in, all the time, sometimes the albums I loved the best got left behind for a while. That was probably for the better, since it meant I wasn't listening to them until I was sick to death of them, either. But when I heard one after so long, like this one, it brought back . . . everything I associated with those songs. A visceral, overwhelming rush of feelings and memories and smells and sights, emotions welling up, like being transported back in time.

I remembered when this album came out. High school had ended a few weeks before. I'd listened to this in the summertime, while lying in my mom's backyard, the grass tall around me. I'd put on headphones and stared up at the sky and watched the clouds and gotten lost. I'd been trying to figure out, then, what I wanted to do with my life. My mom had urged me to go to college, and I'd taken a few courses, but I'd already known that probably wasn't for me. Not then. It had been a weird time, stuck somewhere between pleased and thrilled at being an adult and scared out of my mind, confused and concerned about what would come next. But for a while, I'd let myself escape into music, let my mind work out things without pushing them.

That fall, at one of the courses I was taking, I'd met Tuck. We'd hit it off, for whatever reason. He'd told me he was in a band, and that they were looking for someone to help haul their gear around when they played local shows. I'd told him I was looking for a job. I'd been with them ever since. What had started as part-time, something to do while I searched for other, steadier options, had become full-time, my career, and any ideas I'd had about finding what I really wanted to do with my life had disappeared. This was it. It definitely wasn't everyone's idea of a dream job, but it suited me. I was good at it, and it made me happy. I didn't think there should really be anything more to a dream job than that.

And all of that, somehow, had gotten wrapped up in the twelve songs on the album we were listening to. Hearing them made me remember. Or not remember, but they made me feel for a few minutes like I was in both places, both times. Scared and secure. Young and not so young. Confused and sure. Just starting out, and comfortably settled into my life.

Beside me, Nick was quiet, listening. He was holding the album cover between his hands, like he'd held the record itself, the edges balanced against his palms. He'd been reading the lyrics printed on the inside. But I didn't think he was anymore. He'd gone still in the way that meant tension or deep thought or emotion.

I turned to him, just enough so I could see him. He glanced up at me and smiled, but the smile was tight and lopsided.

"It's weird, isn't it?" I asked. "Hearing it. Like . . . you're in two places at once."

He nodded, and ran his fingers up over the edge of the album cover. "I didn't think my life would be like this."

"Is that a good thing or a bad thing?" I asked, so soft I wasn't sure if he'd hear my voice over the music.

His smile went slightly wider, and it lost that tightness. "Good. I think. Yeah."

He set the cover down on the floor in front of him and twisted around to face me. "I'm glad you're here. I'm glad . . . I got to see you again. I know you maybe aren't. Maybe you wanted whatever happened between us to stay in the past. But I wasn't . . . I wanted to see you again. Talk to you. And I'm happy this worked out like this."

I took a deep breath. "I didn't want it to stay in the past. I didn't . . . want it to be over. It just . . . was."

He didn't move, but something about the way he was focused on me felt like he had turned to face me more, like he had opened himself up to me. "And now?"

I shook my head. "I don't . . . I don't know how anymore."

"Oh. That's simple." He leaned forward, resting his weight on his hands, braced against the thick carpet, and kissed me. It was soft and easy, undemanding, but he didn't pull away quickly, either. He kept going, let his lips move slowly and gently against mine. And I kissed him back.

I'd thought about kissing Nicky. I hadn't actually imagined it would happen again, but I'd daydreamed about it. I'd tried to remember the way he'd tasted, how his hair had slipped through my fingers. This wasn't the same. And it wasn't the same as the last time I'd kissed him, either. This was all new, like we were different people now, and everything we'd learned about each other before had to be relearned. There was a hint of awkwardness in the kiss, and uncertainty, a holding back, like we were both trying to figure out what the other wanted. But mostly, after the hesitancy, under the caution, the kiss was just good.

Nick pulled back after a minute. The kiss had gone on longer than I'd expected. We weren't quite out of breath, but Nick's lips were plump and red, and I was probably flushed. I could feel the heat rising up in my face. I'd tucked my hands around Nick's jaw, my fingers behind his ears, so his hair fell over them, and I couldn't quite make myself let go.

He smiled at me, lazy and sweet. "See? It's simple."

It was. It was so simple. So easy. It would be the easiest thing in the world, to lose myself for a little while in this man. To let him take everything away.

"I . . ." I flexed my fingers, pushing them further into his hair, and he arched into the movement like a cat. His eyes flickered closed, and it was . . . sexy, but more than that, it was intimate. Not a gesture a hookup or a one-night stand made. It was almost like a surrender, something personal, all contained in that simple tilt of his head. I let my fingers trail down, along the slope of his jaw, down his neck, and he tipped his head back to let me. God, it was only fingertips on skin, and it was startling in how close it made me feel to him, in the way it turned me on, to watch him react to being touched by me.

"I don't . . ." I tried again, but I didn't know what I was trying to say. "I don't know how to do this."

He reached up and caught my hands, and brought them down to rest on his crossed ankles. His eyes blinked open and he stared at me.

"Do what, Quinn?"

"What we had before . . ." I tightened my fingers around his, the movement reflexive, and he squeezed back. "What we were doing . . ."

He squeezed my hands again, and then let go. "We didn't have anything," he said. Gently. So gently, but it cut me right to the quick, because he said it in a way that made it the absolute truth. "We might have. But we went our separate ways before it could happen. Now it's been a year since I've seen you. There isn't anything left from that."

I swallowed. "Nothing?"

I didn't know why I was asking. I hadn't let myself think about wanting this. Not after I'd as good as stood him up a year ago. Not when I was . . . messed up, my brain wanted to supply, but that wasn't the right term. I wasn't messed up. My brother had died, and I was slowly coming to terms with that, putting my world back together, and things were . . . okay. But they weren't what they'd been before, would never be the same, and I was scared. Scared that I didn't know how to do this anymore. Didn't know how to be with someone, even like this.

A smile flickered over his mouth, enough to turn his lips up at the corners, to make his eyes crinkle. "Maybe not nothing. I did really want to kiss you again. I remember it being like this before. Always wanting to touch you."

I leaned toward him. No conscious thought. I only wanted to respond to that, to what it did to me, in the most physical way. He didn't seem to be adverse to the idea. He leaned with me, his hands sliding up my neck this time, to cup my head. I dropped mine to his waist. He felt so solid and so fragile at the same time, his bones and muscles shifting beneath my palms. I knew, from before, that if I pulled him to me, he wouldn't feel small against my larger frame, but I would still have that odd, unfathomable desire to protect him, to cradle him.

He inched forward the last little bit, and we kissed again. It was heavier this time, mouths open, breath blending, the heat and warmth and closeness of it crowding out every other thought in my brain. We kept tugging at each other, moving closer and closer across the space of carpet that separated us. His knees bumped mine, and then he rose up so he was almost kneeling over me. In a distant part of my brain, I figured it probably wouldn't be much time before he was in my lap. Before I got to feel that mix of his strength and grace pressed up against me.

There was a noise at the door, which I ignored, dismissing it as unimportant when I was getting lost in how salty and warm Nicky tasted. Then someone cleared their throat, sharply, and said my name.

I jerked back from Nicky, but I couldn't really get too far from him with my hands all over him and him practically on top of me. I blinked up into Nick's face, and then we both turned at the same time to see who had spoken.

It was Ava, standing almost like Nick had earlier, her shoulder pressed to the doorframe. Her arms were crossed over her chest, but she didn't look angry. She looked amused, although I was pretty sure she was doing her best to hide the expression.

"Hey, Nicky," she said, and I had to admire the way she made her voice come out normal.

"Hey." He swallowed, but he didn't move and didn't take his hands off my shoulders. There was a deep red blush rising up his neck, but he stared right back at Ava like she hadn't just caught him in a precarious position. Not that it was that precarious. I was pretty sure we weren't the only musicians or crew who had had the urge to get busy in one of the studio's back rooms.

"That was a really nice drum track you put down this morning." She'd completely managed to get rid of any amusement. "Ty let me listen back. Really cool direction you went with it. I like your snare sound."

He sat down a little, putting some of his weight on me. "You should come see the new kit I got. You'd like it a lot. You'll want one for yourself."

She laughed, full and loud. "Quinn'll kill me if I want to start hauling a second kit around."

Nicky laughed too, and any tension that might have been in the room dissolved.

"We're gonna get dinner and bring it back. Ben said there's some taco place that's the best . . . You two want to join us?" She did a very good job of not staring at where my hands rested on Nick's hips, or raising her eyebrow, or otherwise hinting that maybe we didn't want to join her because we were *very busy*.

But the fact was, if I was going to fuck Nicky again, I was pretty sure I didn't want it to be on the hard floor of a semiforgotten room in an underground recording studio. I was already getting a cramp from sitting like this. And anyone could walk in on us, as Ava had proven.

And I wasn't, when it came right down to it, sure I wanted to fuck Nick again. Well, I did. I most definitely wanted him, in every way possible. But I wasn't sure it was a good idea. I wasn't sure . . . I could handle it.

I turned back to Nick and skimmed my hands down his thighs. Not intimate, only a caress, something that wouldn't be uncomfortable with Ava standing there. I hoped the touch would tell him I wasn't backing out, or saying no. Just that I needed a bit of space. "Should we head upstairs?"

He stared at me for a second, like he was studying me. Then he nodded. He bounced upright, the movement casual and easy and fluid, and I had to stare at him for a second, in awe and envy. Then he was reaching a hand down for me, like he'd done a few days before when we'd sat on the grass and I'd told him about Eric, and I took it so he could pull me up beside him.

Ava chattered away about music and drumming and what cymbals Nick was using while we walked back upstairs. Ava was . . . definitely not the most calming person I'd ever met. Her thoughts danced around at about a million miles an hour and were usually spilling out of her mouth before she thought about them. But there was something about her that was soothing. That made things comfortable. Maybe it was the ease with which she regarded her own awkwardness. She knew she wasn't what people expected, and she didn't care. Or she'd learned not to care as much. And knowing she was going to be herself made everything else simpler. So there wasn't any weirdness, walking up to dinner, having just kissed Nick in a way that had definitely been leading toward more than kissing. Her chatter didn't let anything like that touch us.

Dinner was fun and casual, like we'd been doing for the past few nights. Bellamy and Micah and Ben had gotten the tacos and sides and whatever everyone else had decided we needed to have, and it had all been put in the middle of Ben's big table so we could fill up a plate with whatever we liked. Then we sat around the kitchen and the living room.

Nick and I didn't sit next to each other. I didn't think it had happened on purpose—I certainly hadn't designed it that way, although I was a little relieved to let some of the heat and tension and want between us cool down. But Bellamy had snagged Nick when we came in, and I'd gotten caught in a conversation with Elliot and Danni, and sticking together hadn't happened. I kept glancing over at him, though. I couldn't help it. Even when I couldn't see him, I could feel him. As if kissing him had restarted some internal tracker that was specifically designed to alert me to Nicky.

At least half the time, when I glanced up and sought him out, he was already staring back at me. We'd both look away. Embarrassed, maybe. Or simply wanting to be private. I wasn't sure. I wasn't hiding it from anyone, necessarily, but I wanted to keep this, whatever it was, to myself. For now. But the seconds during which our gazes held got longer, and longer, until the glances lingered, and it was like I could feel him on my skin, like his presence was a pleasant weight.

Nothing else happened between us. Just all that staring, and the memory of him in my lap. It got late and our miniature party broke apart. Bellamy and Micah disappeared into their bedroom. Ava went out on the back porch to call her girlfriend. Ty, Tuck, Ben, and Rest in Peach's producer got involved in a discussion about the progression of recording over the years, how much it had changed. Eventually, Danni made them stop talking so they could go home—apparently Danni was Ty's ride. Nicky was Elliot's, so Nick didn't stick around too much longer after that. They said their good nights, and Nick shot me one more hard, hot glance that felt like a promise, if I was being either hopeful or terrified. Then they all headed out.

The living room had gone quiet. Tuck was in a corner with a guitar in his lap. Ben sat beside him. Every now and then one of them would say something to pick their conversation back up. But mostly Tuck played and Ben listened.

I was listening too, getting lost in the random notes. Tuck was playing without pausing—snippets of Escaping Indigo songs, covers, and stuff I was pretty sure he was making up on the spot. I was considering how weird it would be to lean back against the couch and close my eyes—the answer was probably not weird at all. This was a music studio. No one was going to mind if I let myself drop into the sounds of a guitar and a murmured conversation. But then Micah came and sat next to me on the couch.

I glanced over at him. He was rumpled, but he definitely didn't look like he'd been sleeping.

"I thought you were with Bellamy."

"I was."

I raised my eyebrow, and he raised his right back and smirked. I was going red, I knew it. Micah was an adult, I reminded myself. I didn't need to take care of him. But it was still weird to think of a kid who—when I was feeling really nostalgic or mushy or whatever you wanted to call it—I considered almost like a brother, fucking someone down the hall. Or whatever they'd been doing.

My mind shorted out at that. Nope. I did not need to picture my friends in those kinds of private moments.

"Why did you leave him to come back out here, then?" I kept my voice low so I wouldn't interrupt Tuck and Ben. They were in their own world and probably weren't paying us the slightest attention, but still.

The smile slipped off Micah's face. "I wanted to talk to you." He paused and swallowed, and something inside me tightened. "I saw you . . . I saw you looking at Nick. I saw the way he looked back at you."

"Looked how?" I wasn't sure where the words had come from, but I didn't want to misinterpret this.

"Like . . ." He picked his hand up, flicked his fingers, and dropped it. "Like there was something electric between you. Like there was something *between you.*"

My throat had gone dry. "So?"

He raised both eyebrows this time and widened his eyes, tipping his face forward to stare at me. "So? Quinn. I sat there with you back when I was having a hard time with Bellamy, and you asked me about Eric, you asked . . . all those things. If I'd been in love with him. If he'd been in love with me. I told you so many things, about me, about Bellamy, and you didn't think to maybe mention that you're attracted to men?" He glanced over at Ben and Tuck, then back to me. "Are you? Attracted to men?"

I nodded.

His eyes went impossibly wider. "And you didn't tell me? Why not?"

His voice had risen a notch. Not very much, but this wasn't a conversation I wanted to have in front of anyone. I'd probably be fine having this conversation in front of Tuck, actually, but as cool as Ben was, I really didn't know him. He didn't need to hear my private stuff. "Stop. Come with me." I stood up, and Micah followed me into the hallway. All the doors here were closed. The privacy was probably an illusion—if anyone was up, they'd be able to hear us if they listened. But it was good enough.

I tried to figure out how I wanted to respond to him, considered and rejected a dozen possible options, all in a second. My brain was short-circuiting and I couldn't think. "I didn't tell you because it wasn't any of your business." I hadn't meant to be so blunt, but I hadn't been able to stop the words tumbling out, either. It was the wrong way to say it, though.

Micah took a small step back, rocking on his heels like I'd slapped him. He was flushed and flustered. "I thought . . . I mean, when we had that . . . thing, at my apartment, when you pretty much told me to go and get Bellamy, be a better boyfriend, I thought . . . we had a moment there? Like friends?"

I crumpled my brow up, frowning. I was seriously confused. "We did."

"So . . . don't you think that might have been a good time to tell me you were . . . what, gay? Bi?"

I shrugged. I was pretty sure there wasn't a label for me, but then, I hadn't ever really searched for one, either. I liked what I liked. When I liked it, which wasn't often. "When? In the middle of your crisis, I should have been, 'Oh, by the way, sometimes I like dick'?"

He took a full step back this time, horrified. "Maybe not like that."

I sighed and slumped into myself. "It's not about that, anyway. Not about . . ." I waved my hand. "Dick," I finished, softer. Well, this could not get more embarrassing.

A sigh escaped him, and he nodded. "I know." He brushed his hand back through his hair, letting the short strands fall over his fingers. It startled me, how familiar the gesture was. So similar to the one I did when I was stressed, or nervous. It was a common gesture, I supposed, but there was something about the line of his hand, the way he tugged his hair, that reminded me of . . . me. "I . . . You know what

I went through, with Bellamy. I guess maybe I thought you might want to tell me about yourself? In solidarity?" He held up his hand. "But you're right. It isn't any of my business."

He started to turn away, and I reached out and grabbed his arm, making him turn back to face me.

"Micah," I started, but then I wasn't sure what to say. "I'm sorry. You're right."

"I'm not your little brother," he said, gently. "I'm your friend."

I nodded, even though that stung in an odd, semisweet way. Like it was wonderful and terrible at the same time, to be made to acknowledge that. "I didn't think it would matter."

Micah smiled. "If it matters to you, then it matters."

I was still holding his arm, and I let my hand drop. I wasn't sure what to say to that.

"Also, Quinn." His smile went wide. "Nick? Holy shit." He reached out and tapped my shoulder playfully. "Well done, man."

I snorted. "Like you can talk."

"Well." He puffed up a little bit, his shoulders going straighter. I loved how proud he was of Bellamy. Not, I knew, because Bellamy was rock star attractive, although he was. Or because Bellamy was famous. But because Micah loved Bellamy's heart and his mind. And I liked that he wasn't ever afraid to show how much.

We stood there, grinning like fools for a second. Then Micah sobered. "Did Eric know?"

I took a deep breath. "About Nicky? Or about . . . ?"

"Either."

I shook my head.

"Why not? You know he wouldn't have cared."

I swallowed hard, my throat dry and tight. "I met Nick right before Eric died. And . . . before that, I hadn't ever met anyone I liked enough that it seemed important to tell Eric. I wasn't ashamed," I added quickly. "I'm not. And I'm not in the closet. But it didn't ever seem important. I didn't think . . . there would ever be anyone. And if there was, I figured I could tell him then."

Micah opened his mouth, but then he stopped himself and shut it. It didn't matter. I knew exactly what had been about to pop out. I couldn't tell Eric now. There would be no future when I would get to introduce my brother to someone I was dating and try to explain my sexuality to him. There wouldn't ever be a conversation like that now, because I had left it too late, and now the opportunity was gone for good.

There were a lot of things I wished I'd gotten to do or say with Eric. Things I regretted, things I wished I hadn't held back. I hadn't considered this in particular, though. But Micah was so right—Eric wouldn't have cared who I slept with or dated, or how I went about it. And Nicky . . . Eric would have liked Nicky. He would have liked the way Nick made me smile. The way he made me feel easy and carefree, like everything was simple. I could have told Eric, whether or not anything more ever came of me and Nick after that tour. We could have talked about it.

And now we couldn't.

"I wanted to be there for him," I said, my voice almost a whisper, so low I wasn't sure Micah would hear me. "I wanted to be the big brother. I didn't want . . . to lay anything heavy on him."

"This wasn't a heavy thing," Micah said. "He would have wanted to know."

I knew he hadn't said it to be cruel, but it cut, deeply. "I know."

"I'm sorry." Micah's voice was harsh and rough.

"It's fine, it's fine."

"No, it isn't. Oh god, Quinn. I didn't mean to make it sound like . . . like you'd made a mistake with him."

But it had sounded like that, and it was okay, because maybe . . . maybe I needed to hear it. Maybe I needed to be reminded of that. It was something I told myself, tried to be logical about—Eric had been his own person, a grown adult, and he hadn't needed me to take care of him or baby him. But it didn't stop me from feeling guilty. From wanting to have been there for him in any way possible. It had been my job, whether Eric was an adult or not. No matter how old he got. I was the big brother. Caring for him, making sure he was okay, was my job.

I swept my hand over my face, trying to gather myself. It didn't work. "I don't know how . . . how to be with anybody anymore," I admitted, my voice low. Micah took a step forward. "I don't think

I want to have that . . . responsibility on me. Because I'm not good at it. At caring about someone. At taking care of someone. I forgot how."

Micah touched his fingertips to my arm again. "Is this about Nick? Or something else?"

I took a deep breath. "I don't know. Neither." I had to stop this. I couldn't lay this on Micah, or anyone else. This was my own shit, for me to deal with.

"Quinn," he said, drawing out my name.

I gave him a wobbly smile. "I'm fine. Just tired. It's been a long day and it's getting to me."

He nodded slowly, but he still looked skeptical. Like he was trying to peer through me and decide whether I was telling the truth. "You're good at taking care of people, Quinn. You take care of me all the time." He waved his hand around, taking in the studio, but maybe he meant more the band, and the way I'd gotten him the job, and Bellamy.

I didn't think that was really true. Micah took care of himself. He was talented and he made things work for himself. I didn't have anything to do with that. But instead of arguing with him, I reached out again, this time to gather him up into a tight hug. I didn't think I'd ever hugged him before, or touched him in a way that could really be considered close. Not even at Eric's funeral. We'd shaken hands, and done an awkward standing-close-to-each-other-but-leaving-space thing. But this felt right, and Micah went along with the hug, wrapping his arms around me and squeezing the daylights out of me. I always forgot how big he was. I had proof right in front of me on a daily basis, but I still thought of him as a scrawny kid with big feet, who hadn't yet grown into his body. But he was as tall as I was, and built, and he felt strong and warm when he held me.

We let go and stepped back from each other, and it was, if possible, even more awkward. I pushed at his shoulder, turning him around, pointing him toward his bedroom door. "Go. Go be with your boy. I'm fine, I promise."

He nodded and, after one more backward look at me, went off to find Bellamy. I headed in the opposite direction. There was still soft guitar music spilling from the living room. I glanced in and saw Tuck by himself. He had his phone next to him, and he was talking, so I figured it must be on speaker. A second later I heard a light, high woman's voice, and realized he was on the phone with his girlfriend. He laughed at whatever she was saying, and when his head tilted up, he caught my eye. I smiled and waved, and he nodded back.

I kept walking to the room we shared. When had we all paired off so neatly? Well, when had everyone but me paired off so neatly? Not that it was always neat. Everyone was happy, though, for the most part. In love. Everyone had someone they could count on.

That had been me, not so long ago. I'd been the person everyone in Escaping Indigo counted on. I'd been the person Bellamy asked for when he was practicing a piece of music, the one Tuck looked to when he needed someone to listen to him when he got angry or frustrated. I'd been that guy, the guy holding stuff together, the guy people turned to. Now I wasn't. It wasn't a bad thing. Everyone needed that particular one or two people who held them together, who supported them, in a way no one else did. Tuck, Ava, Bellamy, and Micah all had that now. It was just that I didn't. I didn't have a person like that, and I wasn't that person for anyone anymore, either.

I didn't want to take away from that by being envious. I was thrilled for them. They were my friends, all of them, and I couldn't remember ever seeing any of them this . . . alive and happy and just fucking glowing from within. Maybe when they'd gotten the record deal. But this was a different type of happiness. This was simple and overwhelming at the same time, lasting and deep and intrinsic to who they were as people. It was almost awing to see.

Wanting that wasn't something I was sure of. It should be obvious, should probably be something everyone wanted. But I'd seen how much work it took. And I didn't honestly know if I was capable of that.

It was dark, but I didn't bother to turn on any lights in the bedroom. I shut the door, blocking out the light from the hall, but there was enough moonlight coming in through the windows that I could get undressed and find a pair of sleep pants to put on. I climbed into bed, pulling the sheets up over me.

Trying not to think about the things Micah had said was impossible. Micah was right. I should have told Eric, if for no other reason than it was a part of me, and he should have been the person to know all those parts of me. But I hadn't, and now I never could. Just one more way I'd fucked up with him.

Not thinking about Nicky wasn't something I could do, either. Nicky, his weight on me, his tongue in my mouth, the way his fingers dug into my shoulders. How much I wanted it to happen again. And how nervous it made me. Because it felt different this time. It felt like a conscious thing—not a purely physical attraction, not something brought on by proximity. But something we might, consciously, carefully, decide to try again. Maybe it was because this would be the second time. Maybe it was because this time it was more deliberate. Maybe it was because, being together again, by accident, felt a tiny bit like fate.

I closed my eyes and tried to go to sleep. It took a long time.

# chapter five

X

In the morning, when I walked into the kitchen to grab a yogurt for breakfast, Micah met me with a cup of coffee, done with exactly the amount of milk and sugar I liked.

"I'm sorry," he said, soft enough that probably no one else could hear. Ava was sitting at the table, and Bellamy was at the island, watching us. I doubted Micah had told Bellamy what I'd said—he wouldn't have—but I bet Bellamy had some idea of what had happened anyway.

I took the coffee out of his hands, wrapped mine around the hot mug. "It's okay. It's fine."

Micah shook his head, more at himself than at me. "No. I mean, I thought about it. Eric . . . he wouldn't have cared. Like, that stuff, it didn't mean anything to him. He was . . ." He waved his hand in the air, almost over his head, and I got what he meant. Eric had been . . . different. Wrapped up so tightly in music it was like sometimes I couldn't see the person underneath. Like he had existed on a separate level, and normal human things weren't part of his day-to-day. Like Micah had said, stuff like that wouldn't have bothered him because it wasn't in his realm of thought.

"I messed up in a lot of ways with him." I didn't mean the way Eric had been—I hadn't ever wanted him to change, hadn't ever wanted him to be someone else.

Micah sighed. "Bellamy says I have a habit of sticking my nose where it doesn't belong."

I glanced over at Bellamy, who was very carefully staring at his piece of toast. But I caught him watching us out of the corner of his eyes. I turned back to Micah. "You mean, he thinks that because you stuck your nose in *his* business."

Micah shrugged. "Probably."

"Worked out pretty well for him, didn't it?"

Another small shrug, and a slightly embarrassed smile. "I guess it did."

I patted his shoulder and raised the coffee cup in thanks. "Don't worry about it, okay? Don't think about it again. I'm fine."

Micah didn't look completely convinced, but he nodded reluctantly, and when I moved around the island, he went back to Bellamy. They started up a hushed conversation, heads close together.

I went over to the table and sat down next to Ava. She didn't pick her gaze up from where she was contemplating her half-full mug.

"Gonna drink the rest of that?" I asked, half-curious and half-nudging her to do it.

"I know," she said, sounding almost annoyed. She really wasn't a morning person.

"You recording drums today?"

She shook her head, the movement exaggerated. Then she straightened her shoulders and stared right at me. "Hey. I caught you kissing Nicky in the studio yesterday." A slow smile crept across her face.

God, my cheeks must be on fire. If Bellamy didn't know before, he sure knew now. I was desperately glad there wasn't anyone else in the kitchen to overhear her.

"Yeah, you did."

She blinked, and I hoped the caffeine was kicking in. "You going to go for that?" she asked, only a bit softer.

I pulled in a deep breath. "I don't really . . . We're only here for a few more days."

Her eyes narrowed, and I was pretty sure she was waking up now. At least a little. She took a long sip of her coffee. "And we only live a couple hours away from him." She lowered her voice some more.

I shook my head. "Ava . . . I'm not . . ." I loved Ava. She was . . . this constant fixture in my life. Not in a way that meant I could take her for granted, but she'd placed herself in my path and had never stepped out of it. And I'd never tried to walk around her. Had never wanted to. I knew things about her—the way she brushed her teeth before she washed her face, the way she took a long time to wake up, the way she always tapped her kick drum twice, once soft, once hard, to get a feel for the sound before she played, the particular type of green salsa she liked on her tacos—that only a handful of other people knew. I'd lived with her for months at a time, taken care of her, gotten her to work on schedule, made sure she had whatever she needed. We were close in ways I couldn't begin to describe. But we didn't really talk. I didn't really talk to anyone. It wasn't my thing. And I didn't think I could start doing it here and now, either.

"You are," she said, quickly, although I was pretty sure she had no idea how I'd been trying to end that sentence. *I* didn't know. "You deserve something good, Quinn. You deserve a little bit of happiness that's just yours."

She stood up, not giving me any chance to reply. She wandered over to the coffee maker, running her hand across first Bellamy's shoulders, then Micah's, on her way. She filled up her cup, dumped in an ungodly amount of sugar, and headed straight down the stairs to the studio.

I glanced over at the guys. Bellamy raised his eyebrows at me. Micah was hiding a laugh behind his hand. "I love her," he mumbled, and Bellamy leaned over and kissed his forehead.

I might as well head to the studio too. I told Micah and Bellamy I'd meet them there, and made my way down the stairs. Music was already drifting up from below, which was unusual. Someone must have left a door open somewhere, because the place was otherwise pretty well soundproofed. I couldn't tell if the music was Rest in Peach or someone from Escaping Indigo. It was muffled and indistinct, and I followed where it was loudest, until I came to the closer recording room. Escaping Indigo, then. As I came up, someone shut the door. I could still hear the music, now that I was this close, but it was much softer. I stepped into the room with the soundboard, then shut the door behind me, closing all the sound in with me.

It was Tuck, playing around on a guitar. Ava was settling behind her drum set, placing her coffee by her high-hat pedal. She stayed quiet while Tuck played, moving her seat around, getting comfortable, and picking up her sticks. Then she found a measure where she could come in on the one. They played something I hadn't ever heard before. I was pretty sure they were making it up mostly on the spot from the way they watched each other, careful of the other's cues. It was a graceful, precarious dance, without words or even too many gestures. Without ever pausing, missing a beat, or stumbling. A practiced thing that was completely unpracticed. Something that went beyond body language and sound.

I turned away from that two-thirds of the band, and went to sit on the couch in the back of the room. But someone was already sitting there.

Nicky wasn't watching Tuck and Ava. Or maybe he had been, but when I saw him, he was already staring right back at me. He patted the cushion beside him, and I moved without thinking, like he was a magnet. The couch was slightly elevated, so when you were sitting on it, you could still see over the soundboard. I stepped up, then sat beside him. Maybe not as close as his "come here" gesture had indicated, but pretty close.

"Are you not recording or something this morning?" I asked, because it was safe, and because I didn't know what else to say.

He shook his head and threw me a smile. "No. I did scratch tracks last night. They'll record over those today. Then I'll do the final take later."

"Shouldn't you be there?" I realized, as soon as I said it, that it came out sounding like I wanted him to leave. I curled my hand into a fist on my thigh, willing myself not to say anything else and make everything awkward.

Nick shrugged. "I'll go back in a while. I wanted to hear what you all were doing, though. I haven't gotten much of a chance."

"Oh." There was something I was feeling, some tightness or discomfort I couldn't quite name.

But Nicky could, apparently. His smile softened, went gentle and kind, and he reached out so he could touch the side of his hand to mine on the couch cushion. "Also, I wanted to see you again. And I didn't want to go searching through back rooms to find you."

"Oh." The word sounded completely different this time.

"Yeah. Um." He glanced up at me, then back to Ava and Tuck. "I really liked that, yesterday." His gaze was still fixed firmly straight ahead.

There were a thousand things I could say to that. Maybe more. Complicated things and things that would define this, and things that probably needed to be said. But there was only one real, simple truth. "Me too."

His smile, which had faded away as he spoke, bloomed big and bold and bright on his face again. He turned to catch my eye. "Oh, good." Then the expression slipped. "But I don't . . . I didn't mean to bring all the . . . relationship stuff back up, Quinn. I'm sorry."

I nodded. I wasn't sure whether that was a relief or a huge disappointment.

He patted his hands on his knee, fingers moving in time to the beat Ava was playing. He added a little frill with his palm, and she played a quick fill at the same time. I knew it was only about timing, and measures, and the natural counts and lengths in music, how that got ingrained into a musician. But there was something about it, some synchronicity, that seemed like magic.

"Anyway," he said softly. "I'm . . ." He sighed. "I'm glad we have this chance to . . . We used to be friends, I think? And I want . . . I hope maybe we can be that again?"

I nodded, absorbing that. That made sense. That was a place . . . to start from. To maybe end the awkwardness between us. "Maybe we could go out to dinner tonight? Just us?" I asked, suddenly. He blinked, surprised, but I felt almost the same. I hadn't been planning to ask. It had just popped out. I didn't want to take it back, though.

"To talk," I said. "I think we should probably talk. And maybe . . ." I let the rest of the sentence trail off.

He glanced at me, then quickly away. He was picking at the hem of his shorts now, his fingers tugging at a loose thread, and he was staring at his hand, carefully not meeting my eyes. There was a bright blush, high on his cheekbones. It didn't look like embarrassment. It looked like nerves.

"I'm not . . . I know I was the one who started the kiss, but . . ." Nicky said, letting his words trail off.

I shook my head. "Can we just . . . see what happens? Go out to dinner, as friends, and see?" I couldn't lie and say I didn't want another kiss like that, or maybe more. But I wasn't sure *what* I wanted. And I didn't think Nicky knew what he wanted, either. "I'd like to see if we could maybe figure things out. As friends. You and me." I said it gently. I didn't like seeing him nervous. I didn't want to be the cause of that, not ever.

He nodded slowly, then harder. "Yeah, okay. I mean, yes, I'd like to."

Of course, it ended up being me who was stressed that evening when I went to get ready for my . . . what? Date? We were just two guys going for dinner. But it seemed almost like a date. It felt like it was important.

And I could still picture the blush on his face, the nervous twitch of his fingers, his focus anywhere but on me when I asked and he decided how to answer.

And I could still feel him in my arms, that refreshed memory, something I'd never thought I would get to have again. There was something between us, still, whether either of us was sure what it was yet or not.

So maybe we actually were going on a date. Maybe we weren't. It almost didn't matter. I was going to be tense either way, and either way, I wanted to look good. Wear the right thing. Whatever that was.

This was a harder challenge than I'd imagined, though. It wasn't like I'd brought any nice clothes with me to a recording studio, knowing we were going to be hanging out and catching quick meals after long days. T-shirts and shorts and jeans and a couple of hoodies in case it got cold. That was basically always my wardrobe, and it had never occurred to me that I might need something else. Not for this trip, at least.

Ava wandered into my room and sat on my bed, her phone in her hand. I was standing in the bathroom and could see her reflection in the mirror.

"This isn't your room," I said, half-gentle, half-exasperated.

She raised her head and glanced, pointedly, around the room, at the mess Tuck and I had already managed to make in a few short days. I hadn't exactly helped by strewing my clothes everywhere while trying to figure out what to wear. "I'm well aware," she said, a slight dry edge to her voice.

"Tuck isn't here either."

Her eyebrows crept upward. "I see that."

I dropped my hands to the counter and took a deep breath, then turned around to face her. "Sorry. I'm sorry." I was being a jerk. The nerves were getting to me, and she was being kind enough not to say anything too harsh. "Why are you here?"

She slipped her phone into her pocket, crossed her legs in front of her, and leaned forward. "Tuck said you were in here freaking out. And that you probably needed a girl's help." She held up a hand. "I'm not going to get into how sexist that is. I already told Tuck. He knows better than to say something like that again."

I eyed her up and down. She was wearing a T-shirt with the sleeves cut off and a faded logo emblazoned on the front, and jeans that had holes not only in the knees, but up the backs of her thighs. "I'm not sure you were what he meant by that, either."

She laughed, tipping her head back. "No, probably not. Probably he's hoping I'll call Cara and she can assist you over the phone." Then her expression went more serious, and she lowered her voice, so I knew she wasn't joking anymore. "What's the matter, Quinn?"

I sighed, and plopped down on the other bed. I dropped my hands between my knees. "I asked Nick out. To dinner." I flicked my gaze to hers, then looked away. "And I was trying to find something decent to wear. I'm all . . ." I sighed and shrugged. "I didn't even notice Tuck come in. I didn't see him. I'm . . ." This time I gestured at the clothes.

Ava leaned forward a little bit more, and reached out to tuck a strand of my hair behind my ear. It was too long—not like I'd let it grow out because I liked it that way, but like I'd forgotten to get it cut. It was long enough to have a slight curl, and pieces were tickling my chin and getting in my eyes. Her touch was gentle, pushing the strands back, smoothing out the places I'd ruffled up with my fingers.

"Why do you need something nice to wear to go out with Nicky?" She pulled her hand away and sat back.

I opened my mouth, closed it, tried again. "I think it's a date."

She smiled, softer than before. "I saw Nick earlier. He was, like, floating a fucking foot above the ground. It's a date. Or he thinks it is. Or he's hoping for something from it." She narrowed her eyes. "How can you not know if it's a date if you're the one who asked? Do *you* want it to be a date?"

I hesitated. I didn't know how to answer either of those questions. I shrugged instead. "I don't know. But I do know I want to look good for him."

She blinked, almost comically. The she raked her eyes over me, and I tried to tell what she was seeing. I wasn't hideous. I wasn't vain, but I was pretty sure I was decent looking. My mother had always called me handsome. I hadn't ever been able to tell whether that was because she was my mom or not. She hadn't ever called Eric that, but Eric had been . . . beautiful. I wasn't beautiful. I was rough where he'd been fine. I was unpolished where he had shone. We had the same coloring—his hair had been darker than my brown, but our skin had been the same shade, our eyes had been the same dark green. Different builds, though. I was broad and what some people might have called sturdy or cuddly, and he'd been lithe and wiry. I was scruffy. We'd both had gauges in our ears, but they'd been completely different on him. Maybe because he'd put on makeup to go with them. Maybe because I was hiding mine behind my hair now.

"You always look good," Ava said, bringing me out of my reveries.

"You're attracted to girls."

"I'm *bi*, you jackass." But I could tell she knew I was arguing just to be a dick, and her tone wasn't as angry as it probably should be. "Don't fucking deflect me because you're nervous. Besides, I'm not blind, even if I'm not attracted to you. Which I'm not. But not because you're a man."

I wrinkled my nose. "Thanks, I think?"

She nodded and gave me a smile, more reassuring than teasing, and it made all the places where I'd been holding in my uneasiness come undone.

I slumped. "I *am* nervous."

"Why? This is Nicky. You practically lived with him when we were on tour. You've been out together lots of times."

"Yeah, but . . ." I dragged my hand over my face. "That was all . . . before." I didn't know how to explain any of it, so I decided not to try. "And . . . I like him. I think I like him a lot." And I didn't know what I wanted out of this, or what would happen. I didn't want to say that, though.

She rocked forward again, but not enough to touch me. Her phone buzzed in her pocket, but she didn't make a move toward it. "That seems like a good thing?"

"Just . . ." I wasn't the guy who talked about his feelings. I was the guy everyone else came to, to talk about theirs. I was the guy who listened, and who fixed where I could or offered a shoulder or held someone's hand. I got people what they needed; I fed them; I made them comfortable; I took care of them. That was how I liked it. That was how I worked best.

"This—" I held my hand out and gestured, trying to take in the studio and everything that went with it "—is a lot *more* than I expected."

Her eyebrows drew together. "What is? Nicky? I know you didn't know he'd be here, but—"

"No," I said, cutting her off. "Not Nick. *This*. Being here, watching you guys record, it's like . . ." I swallowed hard. "I keep being reminded of my brother. And I keep wondering what if. I had that all so under control. I was *okay*. But now . . . I keep wondering what if."

"Oh."

"That." I pointed at her. "That sound is exactly why I didn't want to tell anyone."

She stuck her tongue out at me. "What sound? Give me a break. You didn't want to tell anyone because you love bottling up your emotions too much. Don't pin this on me."

And that easily, she took all the air out from under me. "Yeah. You're probably right."

"So what you're saying is that a superhot guy agreed to go out with you, but you got tangled in the past and now your brain is giving you a shit-ton of stuff to worry about."

Well. That was certainly succinct. "Yes."

She smiled again, but this time, it wasn't joking, or teasing, or cajoling, or even very happy. It looked . . . bitter and sad and like maybe she was lost.

"I know about that." She held up a hand. "I'm not saying we're the same, or what we've been through is the same, because it isn't. But I know about letting the past drag you down. I know about feeling smothered by it. Wishing it was different. Wishing you'd changed it. I get that, at least."

I nodded. I wanted to . . . ask her things. Ask her exactly how she knew about that, what had changed for her. What had made her feel that way. Ask how she handled it. Ask her what I should do. Ask for help, or guidance, or maybe a hug, because I really was that confused. But I still couldn't make myself do any of that.

"Let me ask you, Quinn—what do you want out of this?"

"Out of . . . what?"

"Out of tonight. This maybe-date with Nick."

I shook my head. "I don't know." I'd tried to imagine it in progress, but it was mostly fuzz, with wine, and maybe kissing. Or maybe absolutely no kissing. Maybe only talking, like I had said, because kissing was wonderful, but it was scary too. I wasn't sure I could come back from kissing. And I wasn't sure I wanted to figure out how to tackle what came after kissing, all those things and emotions and ties, either. So, nothing set in stone, nothing I was really hoping for, or nothing I'd let myself hope for. Anything too real seemed like too much, too fast, too frightening.

She lifted her shoulders in an easy, lazy shrug. "So," she said, stretching out the word, "just let it happen. This is supposed to be fun. We're here to have fun. Well." She frowned slightly. "I'm working. And . . ." She made a noise that sounded like a grumble at the same time. Her eyes went wide to emphasize her next words. "It's a lot of fucking work. God, I always forget how draining this is. But." She caught my gaze and held it. "You're basically on vacation. We're *here*. This place is amazing. We're in the heart of everything. We can go to the beach. We get to listen to amazing music, and talk music in the nerdiest way possible, and hang out with people who love music." She started to sound a little dreamy before she snapped her focus back to me. "Go out tonight. Have a really good time. Get kissed. That's all you have to do. That's all it has to be, for right now. Only *now*."

I nodded. God, she was right. I didn't have to think about after dinner, or even during dinner. I didn't have to wonder what I'd do about what came after kissing, if anything. All I had to do was *now*. I hadn't had to voice a single one of my questions to her, but she'd somehow managed to answer them anyway.

"I still don't know what to wear." I pointed at the shirt I'd dropped on the floor when she'd come in.

She flicked her fingers, there and there and there, pointing at stuff around the room. "The blue T-shirt with the V-neck. The color's good against your skin. Cleanest, tightest jeans you have. Show off your ass. And put on a jacket. It'll make you look classier, and it'll be cooler once the sun goes down, anyway. I doubt Nicky has any clothes dressier than you do, so that'll work fine. Do you know where you're going?" I shook my head, and she sighed. "I'll google it. Somewhere not too fancy. But nice."

I blinked. "I don't have a jacket. Just hoodies."

"Micah has one. Ask him."

I nodded and stood up to gather the clothes she'd pointed at, holding up my only pair of decent jeans for her inspection. She was kind enough not to make a face at how worn they were. I laid them and the T-shirt on the bed, and started to head down the hall to ask Micah if I could borrow this jacket Ava seemed to think he had. But before I left the room, I turned back to her.

"Thank you."

She shrugged again. "No problem."

"Are you going to answer your text or whatever?" I gestured at her pocket, where I'd heard her phone buzzing before.

She smiled, softer, a more private, turned-inward expression. "In a minute. You get my attention for a little while longer."

I stepped back into the room, and bent down, cupping her face, and dropped a kiss on the top of her head. Escaping Indigo was a pretty touchy-feely band, with each other. They were always leaning on each other or holding hands or kissing cheeks. Even Micah had picked up on that, probably because he was the type of person who liked to be touched a lot, and that closeness worked for him. I hadn't ever really joined in on that, though, because it wasn't me. But if anyone deserved it, at any time, it was Ava, now.

She patted my hand, grinned up at me, and watched me until I left the room.

# chapter six

X

That evening, Nicky and I followed the directions Ava had given me to the restaurant where she'd made a reservation for us. It was perfect. It was a tiny Italian place on a corner, windows strung with white fairy lights and fake ivy, looking out on the street and the foot traffic. It was a hole-in-the-wall, and not pretentious—half the people in the place were sitting at the bar, dressed in jeans and sneakers like we were. But the scents coming from inside, stronger when we stepped through the doorway, were amazing. Spicy and sweet and rich. We got a table right at the window, looking out onto all the people passing by in their fashionable-yet-casual clothes. Beyond that, the sunset: pink and blue and gold as the sun sank over a beach we couldn't quite see. It was like being on stage, but it was private at the same time. A strange counterpoint.

I was worried that maybe Nick would want to start right into a conversation about where we stood and what we were doing together, and I wasn't really ready for that. Or, on the other hand, I was worried we'd try to make small talk, and find we didn't have anything to talk about anymore, a year down the road from when we'd first met. But it wasn't like that at all, in either way. Nick asked something, and the conversation went from there. It was light, but not inane, and never boring. We could still talk about music, and Nick was good at letting one topic slide into another, so by the time we'd eaten and were getting ready for dessert, we'd discussed a dozen different things, shared memories, laughed, and it had never been too strained or awkward. I'd forgotten that about him, probably because he used this semi-superpower in such a background way.

But I'd always been comfortable with him. I'd always felt at ease. It was one of the things I liked best about him.

We ordered dessert, because why not, and when it came, the waiter had brought extra spoons so we could share each one if we wanted to. And there was something about the gesture, about the way my dessert looked on the table, all delicate and pretty, spun sugar and chocolate curls, that snapped me back from the comfortable place I'd been and into the panic I'd started earlier when I was trying to decide what to wear. There was something about ordering dessert that made this feel like . . . a real date.

Nicky looked up at me, spoon in his hand, eyes wide, and I could see the same thing creeping over him. He blushed, like he had when I'd asked him to come to dinner. "Quinn . . ."

God, how was he so sweet? How had I ever gotten this close to someone who blushed like that, and was so earnest, and said my name in a way that was . . . hopeful and kind and nervous, all at once?

"Nick . . ." It was ridiculous to ask this. But I didn't think, suddenly and all at once, that I could get through another minute sitting across from him without knowing. "Is this a date?" I felt like a confused teenager. I felt like an idiot.

He laughed, not unkindly. Almost self-deprecatingly. "Don't you get to decide that?"

I shook my head. "I don't think so. I think it has to be mutual."

"Do you want it to be, though?" he asked softly.

I wasn't sure. I really wasn't. Part of me did want that. If I dug deep and poked at the secret places of my heart, then I knew that I did. I'd liked kissing him yesterday. I'd liked having lunch with him. I'd liked simply *being* with him, the way we had been before, when Rest in Peach was on tour with Escaping Indigo. I'd missed that, and I'd forgotten how much. Or I'd tried to tell myself it hadn't been as awesome as it had seemed at the time.

But I couldn't deny it, now that Nicky was here with me again. We were good together, and when he'd been my friend—when we'd spent all that time flirting, but also all that time hanging out and getting to know each other—I'd been . . . happy. Purely happy. It had been so good. And it felt just as good now, if one hundred percent more confusing and fragile.

I couldn't deny that the kissing had also been very, very nice. That I wanted more of it. But it made things real, and frightening, and big.

I also knew I didn't want to disappoint him, the same way I'd known I wanted to look good for him tonight. And that was probably enough to constitute a date right there.

I nodded, then hesitated and wobbled my head back and forth in uncertainty. "I didn't mean for it to be when I asked you to come with me. But now I'm not sure. I want . . . what you said, about being friends. About seeing where we stand. I want that. I hate it that everything's awkward between us. We were good together, as friends. And . . ." I trailed off and took an unsteady breath. We had been good together as friends, and we'd been good together as lovers. "Is that okay?"

He took a deep breath of his own, and let it out slowly. "There's this song I love, about how . . . if you fall for someone, it's your choice. About how . . . if you miss them, later, it's your fault. I thought of that song a lot after the last time I saw you, Quinn. I kept wondering what I'd done wrong. Why it hurt so much that you never called."

He smiled, probably to gentle the words, but I cringed. I hadn't ever wanted to make him feel like that. But I'd been too wrapped up in myself to notice.

"I kept telling myself," he continued, "that if I missed you, if it hurt, it was no one's fault but mine. You didn't make me start to fall for you. It just happened, and I let it. And it hurt more than I'd expected it to, when it was over." He pressed his lips together, as if he was trying to decide what to say. "It helped, actually. It made me less angry." He closed his eyes, went quiet for a minute. When he opened them, he stared right at me, without flinching or glancing away, and I did my best to hold his gaze. "I'd like to try again with you, Quinn. I would. But if I start something with you . . . I would be foolish to, when I know you're capable of hurting me that way. That would be my fault too. More, this time."

I swallowed. I wasn't sure, for a second, if I'd be able to get any words out. But then I did. "So what are you saying?"

"I'm saying . . . let's just see what happens? Let's not promise each other anything, or make any plans except for what's right in front of us. That was where we messed up last time. I thought it might be serious, and you . . ." He huffed out a laugh, and that soft sound cut directly into all my tender places. "I don't know what you thought, but serious wasn't what it turned out to be. I don't want to set either of us up for disappointment again. So let's . . . have fun? Relieve some tension." He gave me a comical leer, surprising a laugh out of me. Then his expression went serious. "I'm not going to lie and say I don't want to try again. I never wanted to stop, really. But I don't want the same outcome. I want us to be okay, and I want us to be okay with each other. So let's see how these few days go, and focus only on that. Take it a step at a time. Okay?"

I nodded slowly.

"And if it doesn't go any further than that," he added, his words careful, like he was selecting each one for precision, "if it doesn't work out, then neither of us will be hurt. Is that okay?"

I nodded again. It was almost like what Ava had said. Only think about the present moment, and nothing past it. It made things simpler, for sure. Uncertain, but simpler. Safe.

"Okay," I answered. "Is . . . is it really okay with you?"

He laughed, but he didn't answer. Instead, he said, "You're . . . perceptive, I think. Awfully perceptive."

"No, I'm not." I was good at reading people I knew. Or I had been. Once, a long time ago. I'd thought I was. I'd thought I'd been good at knowing what people wanted or needed, and making it happen for them. But I hadn't ever known what Eric needed. I hadn't seen any need in him at all. So obviously that talent was a lie.

Nick waved his hand. Then he took a deep breath and met my eyes. "I'm just scared."

I almost dropped my spoon at the bluntness of it.

He trained his gaze back down at the plate in front of him. "I know we weren't . . . that we weren't really together or anything, before. And that was fine," he added quickly. He made a quick motion with the spoon. "I didn't expect anything. But I did like you. And I did think we might have had something that was . . . that could have grown past that. That could have been more than those few weeks."

"Nicky . . ."

He glanced up and smiled softly at me. "I'm not saying you broke my heart, Quinn. But it did hurt. I spent a lot of time afterward, wondering what I'd done wrong. I don't want to go through that again if I don't have to. Not with you."

I had no clue how to respond to that. I didn't know what I wanted to say. To reassure him that wouldn't happen because I was in no place to be starting anything with anyone? To promise him I wouldn't hurt him, and ask him for . . . what? Another chance? Did I want that? I might. I'd missed him. But I wasn't good at this. I wouldn't be good for him, wouldn't be able to be what he wanted. It would be a bad idea to pretend I could start anything real. But part of me wanted to argue that I could be that. That I could do better, even though I knew I couldn't.

"I didn't ever mean to hurt you," I said at last. "But I did, and I'm so sorry for it."

He nodded. "Okay. I can live with that."

It seemed like maybe he wanted to end this piece of the conversation, but I wasn't quite ready to.

"I wouldn't do it again," I added. "I mean, I would try very hard not to. But I don't . . . I don't really know where I am. What I'm . . . doing." That was completely inadequate, and didn't actually say anything, but Nick was nodding as if it made perfect sense.

"I think you can't honestly say you can promise me that right now, Quinn. Maybe not ever."

That was blunt too, and it made me ache. But I couldn't deny it, not really. He was right: I couldn't promise that. I couldn't promise I wouldn't hurt him. I couldn't promise that I would do a good job of taking care of him, whether this lasted only the few days we had together, or beyond. Because I'd failed before. I'd failed so hard, in the most important ways. Not only Nicky, but Eric, and maybe the band. There might have been a time when I could have told Nick I'd be there for him, that I could be what he needed, and believed it with my whole heart. But that time was gone, and I wasn't sure it would ever come back.

The plain fact of the matter was, I wasn't capable of doing that anymore, if I ever had been. So I understood why Nicky wanted to protect himself. It made sense, as much as it hurt. And in a way it was a relief, because it took the pressure off. I didn't have to figure out what happened next, where we went after this, what I actually wanted.

We were . . . being in the moment, more or less. As if the studio and the recording time were a magical bubble, a space without rules or a future, ours to make of what we wanted. I liked that.

"I think I'd like to kiss you again," Nicky said softly, tapping his spoon very gently against the porcelain plate. "If we're going to have fun, then I'd like . . . I'd like to be with you in that way. But I know that's asking a lot. To sleep with me, and maybe not have it mean anything later." He flushed bright red and glanced away. "Who am I kidding. It'll mean something to me. I can't do casual sex. I'm not built for it." He flicked his eyes up to mine. "But we could be friends. And maybe we could . . ."

I nodded again. My throat was tight—with desire, with hope, with absolute terror, with heartache. We were already messing this up so bad, by having this conversation, by sitting here together in this ridiculously romantic restaurant. This was all a mistake and it was all going to go horribly wrong because I was going to let Nick down again. I was sure of it. It was what I did. But I wanted to be with him so badly, wanted whatever he'd give me, that I couldn't say no.

"I would like that," I replied. He nodded, and that was the end of the conversation, for now. For a few minutes, a tense silence welled up between us. Then he dipped his spoon into his tiramisu, and made a face of pure bliss, and we were on safe ground again.

We ate our desserts, and instead of putting them in the middle to spoon into them as we pleased, we switched halfway through, swapping plates and bowls. It wasn't the most romantic gesture ever, but there was something companionable about it. Some friendly intimacy that made me want to keep glancing up at Nick, made me want to make this last.

We finished and Nick took the check. I tried to stop him, argued we should split it at least, but he smiled that same goofy, shy grin and told me if this was a date, then he got to pay. So I let him, because the soft way he spoke made me feel mushy on the inside, and I was afraid that if I opened my mouth, something hideously sappy would come out.

Back outside, the traffic on the sidewalk had thinned out somewhat, but not much. There weren't a lot of bars or places like that around here, but there were quite a few restaurants, and all around us people were meeting up with friends, ducking into doors, sitting out on patios that abutted the street. The air was full of conversations, laughter, faint music. It was humid, and warm enough that it seemed to trap the sound around us, make a cocoon of life in this little pocket.

Nicky and I walked close together, our arms bumping. The side of his hand brushed mine, and without thinking about it, I reached out and wrapped my fingers around his, pressed our palms together. It was such a simple touch. Such little contact. But it was like it sparked every nerve in my hand, in my arm, the touch tingling its way up my body in waves. Maybe it was because we were on the street, and anyone could see us, connected like that. But mostly it was just Nicky, just something he did to me.

"My son will be here tomorrow. His mom's dropping him off in the afternoon." His fingers tightened around mine.

"Oh. Right. I forgot." I searched for something more appropriate to say. "That'll be good. Is he . . . interested in the studio?"

Nick turned and smiled at me. "He's two. He's interested in juice and cookies. But I still want him to see. I want him to have . . . any possibility he wants, you know?"

I gave a wobbly nod and a shrug. I didn't really know if two-year-olds were interested in anything outside their own world. But that made sense. "Yeah."

He squeezed my hand again.

"I know I asked you before if you wanted to meet him. Spend some time with us. I know that was . . . before." He waved his free hand between us, taking in the street and the dinner we'd had together. "Like, I meant it as a casual thing. Although, spending time with a two-year-old isn't exactly relaxing. It's probably the last thing anyone wants to be asked to do, actually, when it's not your kid. Or a relation or a kid you know or something. Especially when you're not a kid person . . ."

I laughed, cutting off his winding train of thought. "I don't mind."

He glanced at me. "Seriously, if you're not into it, I get it." He drew in a sharp breath. "But the invitation's still open to hang out with us tomorrow. I'm . . . glad I get to spend some time with you. I'd like to do it some more, while we're here. But tomorrow, that means spending time with Josh too. I'd like you to meet him, if you still want to. I know that's . . . I mean, like I said, he's two. And it's asking a lot. But."

I took a deep breath and let it out. I wanted to say yes. Just say yes and have him be relieved, keep this light, make everything as easy and simple as possible. But I couldn't quite make myself do it. I wanted to follow Ava's advice, only think about tonight, and nothing else, nothing further in the future than that. But my brain was too logical for that, it wanted to plan things out too much. And this was something I simply couldn't make myself take lightly.

"Who will you tell him I am?" I asked.

He sighed, but the sound was thoughtful, not disappointed, and I was pretty sure it had been the right question to ask.

"A friend, probably. I don't think he understands about boyfriends and girlfriends, yet. And that's not what we are, really." Another glance at me, and more of that blush. "And I don't want to tell him anything if it isn't accurate, even if he doesn't get what that means."

I stopped, and the movement stopped him too, turning him to face me. We were standing in the middle of the sidewalk, but the foot traffic was thinner here, closer to the neighborhood, and we weren't too in the way.

"Why do you want me to meet him?" I still had his hand in mine, our arms stretched slightly between us. His fingers jumped, and I tightened my hold.

He wobbled his head in something between a nod and a shake. "I don't know. Because I think he'd like you. Because I like you too. I thought that might have changed, that maybe I'd be too mad at you for not calling, for . . . forgetting about me." He stared at me, held my gaze, and I wanted to say something completely mushy. I wanted to tell him that I hadn't ever forgotten about him, that everything else had gotten in the way, and I hadn't wanted to tangle him up in any of it. That I still didn't. But I couldn't say any of it.

"But I'm not angry." He squeezed my hand. "Not much. I'm . . ." He sighed, and now he did glance away, and didn't finish his sentence, either. Just let it hang there between us, leaving me to guess what he might have ended it with.

He was . . . what? Annoyed? Hurt? A shiver ran through me.

"Mostly, when you walked into the room that first day and I looked up and there you were, I was relieved. I really didn't think . . . Well, I figured I'd see you again. But I didn't think you'd even want to look at me."

Oh god. "It wasn't you. It was never you. It was me." I realized as soon as I said it how cliché that sounded, how trite and awful. But Nicky was nodding.

"I know. You've said." He shrugged. "I'd like to spend time with you, that's all. I'd like . . . I'd like to get some kind of resolution, one way or another, to what we had between us. Because I know it was short, but it meant something to me, and it's been like this open-ended question ever since. I think this week might be a good time for that." He closed his eyes for a second, maybe trying to steady himself, before he opened them again and stared at me. "And I think you'd have fun with Josh."

"I don't know what you want from me." I didn't know what I wanted from *him*. I didn't know what I wanted for myself, what I could handle and what I couldn't. My voice was raw and soft, a whisper between us. But we were so close, he had to have heard it. "But I would like to meet your son. I would like . . ." God, this was more difficult than I'd have guessed, and I didn't know why. I'd meet his kid. It wouldn't make what was or wasn't between us any different. Except it would. I knew it would. "I want to spend time with you. Yes."

He smiled the smallest bit, and tugged me forward with the hand I still held. His other hand came up to cup the back of my neck. He didn't answer in words, didn't give me a cheesy line, as appropriate as it might be right then. He kissed me instead. Gentler than the day before. A flicker of his lips against mine, and then a pull away to give me space. To give me room to stop him. And when I didn't, the flicker came again, with a little bit more pressure, the slightest hint of demand and want and need behind it.

This time when he pulled back, it was far enough to see my face. We were still connected, his hands on me, mine coming up to rest on his waist. His body nearly aligned with mine, although we weren't quite touching except our palms against skin and clothes. "I want *right now*," he said. "I want to be with you while we're both here.

Like last time. Except, no expectations this time. I want it to be fun. Easy. Only . . . this moment, this handful of days. I want to know if what we had last time was real, if we can still work that way together, or if it was . . . a fantasy we cooked up because we were on tour and everything was different then."

I swallowed. "Didn't we just prove we could?" Maybe we hadn't, though. Yes, we'd just spent the last hour and a half having dinner and talking, and it *had* been easy, and we *had* seemed to work together. And when he touched me like this, when I held him, it all felt so right. But I didn't know if any of that actually meant anything. It meant we still got along, that there was a certain easiness between us, but we'd already known that, in a way. It didn't mean that I could promise we would work any better. It didn't mean that I could actually offer to care for Nick. Especially now, when I knew things about myself I hadn't known then.

When I knew I wasn't as good at caring for people as I'd thought.

When everything I'd imagined I'd had figured out about myself, all the steady pieces of me, had crumbled, and I was trying to rebuild on shifting sand.

Maybe all it meant was that we could still talk to each other. I wasn't sure that was enough.

Nick seemed to be considering if we'd actually proved it, though. He stared at me and chewed on his lip.

"You're right," he said after a minute. "In a way." He shook his head and looked down at the scuffed toes of his boots. "I don't know what I'm doing either, Quinn. I'm pretty lost here. Half of my mind is screaming at me to run as fast as I can from you, because I'm so sure it's all going to turn out exactly like before, and it'd be stupid of me to let it."

I tightened my hands on his waist, squeezing him slightly, drawing him back to me. "And the other half?"

He blinked up at me. "The other half says it'd be stupid not to see if we can be friends. The other half says it won't hurt as much if I don't expect too much." That stung, but I tried not to let it show on my face. Nicky kept talking as if he didn't notice. "The other half wants to take you home and get you into my bed, and make the most of the time I have with you."

My breath shuddered out of me. "God, Nicky. Yes, please. Can we do that?"

He laughed, the sound wild and too loud, this side of hysterical. Then he nodded. But he said, "It's a bad idea."

I nodded. That was the truth. That was so very much the truth. "I don't want it if you don't want it."

He stared up into my face. "But you want it. You want me."

It wasn't a question, but I answered anyway. "Very much."

It was me who leaned forward and kissed him this time. No hesitation, and only a few seconds to see if he'd pull back, to judge if this was what he wanted too. It was rough and hard, openmouthed, with none of the finesse he'd given the earlier kiss. But he didn't pull back. Instead, he groaned into my mouth and pressed himself against me, wrapped his arm around my neck to hold me to him.

It wasn't enough. I wanted more and more and more. But we were still on the street, still practically in the way, and I wasn't really keen on getting arrested for indecent exposure or attempting to have sex on a sidewalk. I broke the kiss and dropped my face to his shoulder, moved my lips to the slope of his neck.

"But you still want to fuck, right?" I asked, the crude words coming out silky.

He shuddered and moaned again. "Yes, please."

I loved that I could do that to him. One of the things I hadn't forgotten about him was how all it took was the lightest touch to set him off, to make him lose control. But not here. This wasn't the place.

I tilted my head enough to see around us—I wasn't ready to move from the hold he had on me, the warmth of him. It was darker here, closer to the residential area, and the streetlights were less frequent. Still too public, but I wasn't sure I could wait until we got back to the studio—by then, maybe my rational mind, or Nicky's, would have taken over and we'd remember that this wasn't a good idea. That we were moving too fast. It wasn't our house anyway, and I was sharing a room with Tuck. But not far ahead of us, on our side of the street, was a tight, close alley between two buildings. It would do.

I stepped back and pulled Nicky with me, and he followed without a question. The alley was cleaner than I'd hoped—no dumpsters or anything. It was too small for that. Just a way to get between the tightly packed buildings. The ground under our feet was gritty, and the brick and stucco walls were rough, but none of that mattered.

Nicky got the hint about where we were, and took over once we reached the alley and had ducked inside. He tugged us farther back, into the shadows where the light from the street didn't quite reach. Then he pushed me up against the nearest wall and plastered himself to me again.

The next kiss went on for a while. Long enough that I had time to run my hands all over his arms, up his back, under his shirt, along his abs and up his chest. Long enough that I got to relearn the taste of him, the way his tongue felt in my mouth. Long enough that I could try to catalog the sounds he made when I bit his lower lip, or when I squeezed my hands down on his waist, or when I pressed forward and I could feel the hard line of his cock next to mine.

The last noise was a harsh, long, low groan that ripped its way out of him and buried itself under my skin, making me go from hot and bothered to *I need you right fucking now*. I grabbed him and spun us around, so he was the one pinned to the wall. Without missing a beat, he let me take his weight, and wrapped his legs around my waist. He was heavy, and I probably wouldn't be able to hold him indefinitely, but right then, as it was, it felt like he was handing me his body and his trust, like he was . . . giving himself to me. It was a crazy, heady sensation, and it made me feel powerful and strong, like my blood was on fire, all molten honey in my veins.

I slipped my hands under his ass to hold him up better, but my body weight, pinning him in place, was doing most of the work. I couldn't get a hand free to undo his jeans, though, and the position was awkward and tight, our bodies pressed almost too close.

"Nicky, I need . . ." I managed to shift one hand more directly under him, and I pawed at the front of his jeans, but I couldn't do it one-handed.

He squeezed me tighter with his legs, making me buck up against him. He had his hands on my shoulders, but he dropped one and helped me get his button undone, and the zip. I was afraid I was going to hurt him, that I'd pinch him or something with the zipper, but he was careless with lust. He shoved at his jeans, hard enough that I wondered if the fabric would tear, but it was too tough for that.

And together, we managed to move them out of the way enough that I could pull the waistband of his boxers down, get my hand inside and around him.

He was hot and sticky damp in my palm. The minute I touched him, it was like the world went still and silent around us. The gentle buzz of cars and conversation from down the street faded away. The urgency of before faded too, because here was my goal, in my hands. The worries I'd had, about whether I should really be doing this here, with Nicky, about what it would mean, and whether we should try to resurrect what we'd had a year ago, all grayed out. Just static, just background noise. All I could hear now was my breath, the harshness of it, mixing with Nicky's panting. All my senses were on the way he felt, the tender, delicate silk of his skin, the pulse of his blood in his veins, the way he smelled, like sex and sweat and night air.

He looked up at me, blinking, then meeting my eyes. I could just make out the brown of his in the dark, flecks of color in the shadows of his face. He sighed, and I leaned forward, pressing my forehead to his so we were breathing the same air.

He didn't say anything. Didn't urge me on, didn't rock his hips. Like he was waiting for me, for whenever I was ready, for whenever I decided that we were going to feel things. I breathed out, and he breathed in.

I moved my hand. A tight circle, slick with his pre-come and sweat. I went slowly. I wanted to explore. I wanted to run the tips of my fingers over all these secret places of his. The veins and the smooth skin. The damp velvet and the softness-over-solidness. I wanted to feel the weight of him in my palm. I wanted to know the exact places to touch that would have him moaning the loudest, what would cause him to toss his head back, what would make his eyelids flutter.

I jerked my hand over him, fast and almost too hard, and he cried out, his body arching against mine, like he was fighting me, except he clung harder and closer, urging me on. I did it again.

"Ahhh, yes, that again, please." His voice was rough and sweet and high and he let the words flow out without any pauses between them.

I did as he asked, alternating the harder strokes with soft ones, feather touches, teasing and exploring. He didn't check his noises at all, and I didn't want to ask him to. It would be so easy to get caught here, to be heard over the traffic. But in that moment, I couldn't make myself care.

It didn't take long for him to come. He cried out as he did, more a wail than anything, and the sound was so raw, so pulled from deep inside him, that I wanted to melt against him, wanted to do anything to hear that noise again.

Afterward, he grinned at me and kissed me again, lazily, his lips soft and pliant. Then he slid his legs from around me and dropped to his feet. I held on to him until he was steady, and even then, I didn't want to let go of him.

"You?" He made a move to reach for me. He still had an arm around my neck.

I shook my head. "I'm okay." I was worked up, there wasn't a question of that. But I wanted . . . I wanted to bask in *him*. In his pleasure. I wanted my part in it, this time, to be about pleasing him. "I want to . . ." I shrugged, not really knowing how to put it into words.

He nodded like he got it. He looked slightly disappointed, but I leaned forward and kissed him again, and when I drew back, he was smiling.

"Thank you," he said quietly.

I laughed. "It was good enough you want to thank me for it?"

His expression sobered. "Yeah." He bit at his lip, which was already swollen and tender looking from where I'd gone to town on it. "It was. And . . . thank you for tonight."

I nodded. I didn't know what to say. That I wasn't sure, still, why I had asked? That I had wanted to be with him again, that the kiss the day before had brought something big and frightening and wonderful back to life in me, and it scared me, but I still wanted it? Because it was like by being with Nicky, by being here, surrounded by music and love and people who were friends, I was going backward, leaping back into the life I'd had before Eric died. But he *had* died, and I hadn't, and I was going along like everything was fine. Like a year had been enough time to get over him. To step into my place, where maybe he should be instead. Making music. Being in the center of recording. Falling a little bit in love.

I pushed the thoughts aside. I couldn't examine them right now, and I didn't want to.

I had a tissue in my pocket, thankfully, and Nicky and I cleaned up. He tucked himself back into his jeans, wiggling around to do it, because skinny jeans were no joke. We checked at the mouth of the alley to see if there was anyone around. It wasn't like we could get caught now, but walking back out onto the street felt a little bit sneaky, like we'd gotten away with something. Which . . . we had. We walked the rest of the way back to the studio in silence, but it wasn't strained. It was companionable, and when we got to Nicky's car, parked in the driveway—the last one still there—he turned to me and smiled.

"I'll see you tomorrow, okay?"

I nodded and stepped forward. I didn't know if we were going to do the whole kiss-goodbye thing, but I wanted . . . I wanted to be close to him again, just for a minute.

"And . . . if you'd rather not hang out with me and Joshua, that's okay. I get it. Kids are stressful."

That wasn't the whole of it, and we both knew it. I was stressed about meeting his kid, definitely—especially because kids were simply not in my wheelhouse. But it wasn't Josh that was worrying me, and I was pretty sure Nick was having similar thoughts. It was that meeting Josh meant something. It was big. I didn't know if I was ready for that. I didn't know what it said about us, Nicky and me.

But on the other hand, if I said no, that cut out one of the days Nicky and I had together, to figure this thing out between us. I didn't want that, either. He was right—we had this time together. Maybe we could make something of it. Get something out of it.

"No, I'd like to," I said.

His smile deepened, curled his lips at the corners. Made him look like I'd given him some kind of gift, like I'd done something great, and I couldn't help loving the idea that I'd put that expression on his face. Especially when he'd been so nervous a second before. He still looked nervous, but it was tempered somewhat now by happiness.

"Okay." We moved forward at the same time, and the kiss was gentle and quick, but I was glad it happened. It made me feel steadier in the midst of all this unsteadiness.

Nick got in his car. He gave me a short wave, and then he was driving away. I walked back into the house in a daze and fell onto my bed face-first. I lay there until it got uncomfortable, going over the night again and again in my mind.

I almost couldn't make sense of any of it. The evening, dinner, the alley, the conversations we'd had, were such a whirlwind in my brain. I couldn't decide if I was afraid—of everything that had happened, how far we'd gone, how completely uncertain everything was—or happy because at least for these few days, Nick wanted to be with me.

Eventually, I decided to think only about what Ava, and Nick himself, had said—only now mattered. I didn't have to think further than that. I got up and took off my clothes. Then I crawled under the covers and willed myself to go to sleep.

# chapter seven

X

the next day started pretty much exactly like every other day. Rest in Peach was taking only the morning to record, with the afternoon off, so they got there earlier than usual, but not by much. I wandered out to the kitchen around nine and rummaged through the fridge—I'd been weirded out doing that at first. It wasn't my house. But Ben certainly wasn't waiting around to feed us and cater to us. He'd given us free rein, and he had other important, techy things he needed to be doing. So it was paw through stuff or starve. The kitchen was always well stocked, though. There was organic hipster-style yogurt there—and it was actually really tasty—and fresh fruit to put on top if I wanted, which I did. And coffee in the pot, with every type of creamer and milk and sugar or nonsugar under the sun.

Escaping Indigo was already in the kitchen, but Micah had gone down with Rest in Peach to listen to them play. After we ate, we trooped down too, and the band spent the rest of the morning polishing new material and getting ready to lay down tracks. Same old, same old—it felt that way, especially after nearly two weeks at this. But they were making progress, and the songs sounded amazing, raw and electric, plaintive and alive.

I kept half my attention on the studio room door, expecting Nicky and his son to show up any minute. I could admit to myself that I was . . . not nervous, exactly, but unsure. I hadn't met very many kids—there were some musicians who toted their whole families around with them, and that was cool if it was what you were into, but our business wasn't really suited to anyone under the age of eighteen. Or maybe fifteen. So the only kid experience I had to go on were me and Eric when we were little. We'd both been quiet and self-contained.

Me because I'd been painfully shy. I'd grown out of it, but it had lasted a long time. Eric because he'd always been too busy inside his own head to project much noise outside of himself, unless he had a guitar and a microphone. And for some reason, I expected that Joshua would be the same way.

I should have known better. Nick was a good person—polite, with all sorts of manners and social niceties built in—but he was always bouncing, always searching for ways to bleed off some of the excess energy running through his muscles. And Josh was the same. Except he hadn't figured out how to control any of it. The first time I saw him, he was running down the main hallway, full pelt, with Nick strolling behind him, casual as anything, a huge, proud grin on his face. I couldn't even take a minute to be distracted by how much he glowed when he looked at his kid, because I was dead sure the kid in question was about to run straight into a glass door.

"Josh, stop," Nick said, loud enough to be heard, and firm, but not harsh. And Josh . . . stopped. Dead still, like he'd been frozen. It was so sudden I thought he might fall over, but he kept his balance—wobbly and precarious, but upright.

It didn't last long. Within a second, he'd turned around and run back to his father, who scooped him up and carried him over to the room I'd been sitting in. Tuck and Ava and Bellamy had wrapped up a song, so they set down their instruments and came over. Ben, who'd been recording what the band was working on, swiveled around in his chair.

My lack of knowledge about kids extended to how to talk to them. I didn't have the first clue. Did you treat them like they were babies and couldn't understand everything, so you weren't lording your adult intelligence over them? Or did you act like they were miniature adults and speak to them that way, expecting that they'd get what you were saying?

It turned out it didn't matter, because as soon as Nick set Josh down, Josh started babbling. Even if we'd wanted to talk to him, we wouldn't have gotten a word in edgewise.

He chattered without seeming to worry about whether his words were coming out clearly. What he had to say was too important for small things like coherency or comprehensibility. It was . . . a flood of sound and impressions. Every now and then, I caught something that was crystal clear, like something about Winnie the Pooh, or something about Nicky or his mother, but otherwise he spoke too quickly and left words out, because they didn't matter to him in his rush to speak. Once in a while, his voice would rise on a question and he'd pause and look around at us. We would all be standing there with our mouths hanging open. I didn't know about Ben, but none of the rest of the band, or Micah, had any experience with kids. We'd all nod and make the right noises when Josh paused, though, because it was obvious he expected an answer. And we certainly weren't going to disappoint him.

It was overwhelming. Of all the things I'd expected to feel, overwhelmed by speech wasn't one of them. It was obvious Josh was smart, that his mind was going a million miles an hour. I had no idea how anyone kept up with it.

It wasn't only the way Josh talked, though. It was *Josh* who was overwhelming. Or maybe not him, but everything he represented. I stood there and listened to him, and glanced back and forth between him and Nicky. And I tried to make this fit, in my mind. That Nick had a kid, that he was standing in front of me, and that I'd agreed to spend the day with them. I hadn't known what I'd feel, meeting Nick's kid, but now it hit me, what it all really meant. Nick wasn't only Nick anymore. He was a father, a person with responsibilities; he was someone whose life centered around someone else.

It was a lot to take in, and it struck me for the first time how truly big that was. I'd considered it before, of course, when he told me, but it was different now, seeing Josh and Nick together. It was more than I'd imagined. The way Nick beamed down at him, the way the two of them were so obviously comfortable together. Nick was a natural at this. He loved it. It was so clear.

I would not be a natural. The few times I'd ever been around kids had been awkward and uncomfortable, and none of them had ever seemed particularly enamored with me. But this . . . I'd agreed to *right now* and the time we had together, and maybe I wanted to see where that would go after, see if we still worked together, but a kid was . . . a lot. A lot of commitment, a lot of responsibility.

And I couldn't help thinking of how easy it would be to disappoint a little kid. How much care they needed, how important it was to provide that, to give them steadiness. I wasn't anything steady. I was uncertainty and hurt and the big, glaring possibility of screwing so many things up. What if I screwed up with Nick? What if I screwed up with Josh?

I couldn't tell if Nick was seeing any of those things on my face. I tried to keep my expression neutral, but I wasn't sure if it was working. Nick was absorbed in Josh, for the most part. But when he glanced up at me, he caught my eye and gave me a smile so gentle and tender that I figured he *must* have seen some of my nervousness, plain on my face. But we were in front of everyone, and it wasn't a good place to talk about it.

I wasn't sure I wanted to talk about it, anyway.

I was relieved when Nick turned back to Josh. He didn't let him ramble on for too long. He crouched down and set his hand on Joshua's shoulder, stemming the incessant tide of words. "Should we go see the rest of the studio?"

I doubted Joshua had any idea about a studio or what there could be to see in it, but maybe Nick had hyped it up, or maybe there was simply a lot of excitement for a kid being in a new place, because he nodded hard, his whole head bobbing up and down. Nick stood—he was too tall to take Joshua by the hand, but he gently set his fingertips on Joshua's head, and Josh seemed to be almost magnetized toward him. Like Nick was the point his personal compass called true north.

Nick turned to Ben. "Do you mind? I won't let him mess anything up."

Ben shrugged in his completely laid-back way. "I don't care. Let him run wild."

Nicky grinned and turned to me. The blush was back, but he was obviously too happy to have Josh with him to let embarrassment or nerves make him hesitate. "If you still want to hang out with us, I'll come get you in a half hour, and we can go for lunch or something?"

I nodded, still a little dazed from the whirlwind that was Joshua. He was already talking again, and he kept at it as Nicky steered him out of the room and down the hall.

When they were gone, we all kept standing there. It was like they'd taken any energy in the room with them. Micah turned to Bellamy and said, "Let's never do that," and Bellamy nodded, almost as hard as Joshua had. Ava, though, was looking like she might be contemplating it. Her expression was half curious and thoughtful, and half soft. I couldn't picture Ava as a mother, but Cara would be great at it.

Tuck was starry-eyed too. But he snapped out of it to say, "So, you and Nick, huh?" And then the entirety of the focus in the room was on me.

"Um." I was the best at witty, clever responses.

Ben frowned like he was trying to put together the pieces of a puzzle, except half of them were facedown. "When did you two find time for that?"

I stared at the floor. I would have scuffed my toes if it wouldn't have only made it all the more mortifying. As it was, I just managed to restrain myself. "We knew each other before. We . . . had a thing before."

When I looked back up, they were still watching me. If I could have dug myself a hole through the floorboards and concrete and right down to the earth, and covered it back up over me afterward, I would have. I wasn't the one on display, usually. I chose not to stand on stage. I stayed in the background because it was safe there. Because I wasn't the guy who wanted all the attention in a room on me. And I wasn't sure what it was about the idea of Nick and me together that made everyone stop in their tracks.

Ava came to my rescue. "Give the guy a break. He can fuck whoever he wants."

Okay, so, not *exactly* coming to my rescue, but I appreciated the sentiment.

"Jesus fuck, Ava." Tuck turned to her and laughed. "Does your girl know you talk like that?"

She sniffed and raised her chin. "My girl likes my mouth just fine, thank you very much." She flicked her gaze to me, and her expression softened. "Leave him alone. Let him have his thing. He deserves it."

Tuck had the grace to blush at that, and Bellamy carefully turned away, so there wasn't quite as much attention on me anymore. "Of course he does," Tuck said. He was staring at me again. "Just . . . I didn't know you were into dating, man."

I gave a half shrug. Going for casual and nonchalant and probably coming nowhere close. "I'm not."

"Oh."

I knew it didn't make any sense, even as the words were coming out of my mouth. "Yeah. Nick is . . ." I sighed, long and slow. It was like somewhere between the time I'd seen Joshua come pelting down that hallway and the time those last words slipped out of my mouth, all my defenses had crumbled or been pushed aside. In the gentlest, most caring way. And I was standing in front of my friends like I had to explain myself—not because they were angry or disappointed with me, but because they were happy for me. That made it almost worse somehow, made me feel more vulnerable and raw. "I like him."

It hit me, each time I said it or thought it, that it was more and more true. Frighteningly, obviously true.

The more I thought about it, the happier I was that I'd asked Nick out. That he'd kissed me. That we weren't awkwardly skirting around having once been together. I wanted him. There wasn't any way I could deny that to myself. If he'd only let me have him for this time, while we were all here, I'd live with that.

Bellamy chimed in this time. "As long as it's making you happy. As long as it's what you want."

I nodded. He sounded so sincere. But they all seemed surprised too. I wondered then how much I let myself fade into the background. Not that I didn't think they saw me. I knew that they did, that they considered me a friend, that they cared about me.

I only gave them the pieces of me they needed, though. The pieces they could count on, the pieces that cared for them, the pieces that made up the guy who was always there, always offering support, always ready to lend a hand or an ear. I wondered if I made it easy for them to forget that I was more than that, that I was a person who got confused and lost and scared the same way they did.

Maybe I wanted it that way too. Maybe I didn't want them to see any other sides to me. Maybe I wanted to hide those pieces of me that were vulnerable and tender and uncertain. Maybe I wanted to stay that slight bit separate, so I'd be safer. I wondered if that was one more way I'd messed up at being a friend, at caring for people. It was possible, I was starting to see, had started to see since Eric died, that all the things I'd thought I was the best at—caring for people, being a friend, being *loyal*—I maybe wasn't very good at after all. That maybe that was all a lie.

I wondered if maybe I had done too good a job of hiding those vulnerabilities. And now I was suddenly human in their eyes again.

And if it was a lie, if I really wasn't good at caring for people— and at this point, I was pretty sure I wasn't—then I didn't know what business I had being with Nicky. Not when he had Josh, and I didn't want to mess anything up there. Not when I'd already hurt Nick so badly without intending to. We'd only been together for such a short time then, and it had gone so wrong. And now I had even less to offer him than I had before. I couldn't care for anyone well. Certainly, I wasn't in any place to be making claims about being able to care for a lover.

Half of me wanted to go running after Nick right now, blurt it all out, and tell him we had to stop. That I couldn't do this. Because even being friends with benefits for a week or two seemed too dangerous. It seemed like asking to get hurt, leaving all that room open for me to disappoint Nicky. But I couldn't make myself. The promise of getting to spend time with him—whether that time was in the studio, or in bed, or hanging out with him and his kid—was a warm spot of light inside me. I didn't want to get rid of it. I was afraid it would self-destruct, burst into flames and burn me, that this was all wrong in every way. But I couldn't make myself take it back.

Ben broke the weird tension, the awkwardness that had descended on us, by clapping his hands softly. "Maybe we can go back through that change from chorus to verse one more time?" The band nodded, already drifting back into the music, and I went to my seat on the couch at the other side of the room again.

A half hour later, Nicky appeared at the door and waved at me until he caught my eye.

I waved at the band then, and Tuck gave me a cheeky thumbs-up. Then I went out into the hall and stood in front of Nick and Josh.

Nick was still grinning, wider than I'd ever seen him. He was flushed—not blushing this time, but like he'd been running. I figured it was keeping up with Joshua that had done it. Josh was quiet now, though. Maybe he'd talked himself out with the members of Rest in Peach. He was staring up at me, like he was waiting for me to do or say something. I tried out a smile.

"How's it going?" I asked him and Nicky at the same time, so it wasn't like I was actually directing the question anywhere in particular.

"Really good, I think," Nick answered, and glanced down at his son. "He was really into all the buttons and stuff. And he likes to sit at my drum kit."

I wasn't someone who found kids cute. I'd always figured it was some personality defect in me, because everyone was supposed to think kids were cute. But they were . . . round and unpredictable and sort of unformed in a way that was nerve-racking. Especially at this age, when they were so . . . little. But I *also* had to admit that the idea of Josh sitting at Nick's kit, with Nick standing behind him, beaming, made my heart do a funny jumpy-squeezy thing in my chest.

"Do you have any plans?" I asked. "For the afternoon?" Maybe they wanted to go out and do something exciting.

Nick shrugged. "Visiting the studio was the exciting part of Josh's weekend. Otherwise, this is just normal for us." He brushed his hand over the top of Josh's head. "We're going out for lunch, if you want to join us?"

I nodded, and we left the studio together. Nick drove us to a super-casual family-style restaurant. Joshua was restless from the minute we got inside, and I was pretty sure that most of the time he'd much rather be running around, terrorizing everyone in the place. Nick took it in stride, though, promising him we'd go somewhere to play later. He coaxed him with French fries, and Josh sat and ate, stuffing them in his mouth with distracted abandon.

I glanced around the restaurant and wondered what everyone who saw us thought of us. Nick with his lean build; his strong arms and colorful tattoos displayed by one of the slightly baggy tank tops he wore while he drummed; the thin, smudged traces of eyeliner around his eyelids. Me with my jewelry and my scruff, my curiously skinny jeans on my not-quite-skinny body. And Josh, chattering away to both of us. Did people think Nick and I were a couple? That Josh was our son? Did they wonder how it was that two guys who were as rock grunge as us ended up with a kid? Did they recognize Nick?

We looked just different enough from everyone else in the place that we stood out. Were they sneaking glances and trying to figure out who we were, like I was sneaking looks at them, trying to figure out what they thought of me? Or, since this was LA, did no one care in the slightest?

Or did they wonder how someone like me ended up with Nick? Did they notice how awkward I was, with Joshua in particular? I didn't really know how to talk to him or get him what he needed. Didn't know how to make him laugh, or how to get him to settle down like Nick did. I didn't know how to take care of him.

I was awkward with Nick too, in some ways. I didn't know where we stood with each other—didn't actually want to know, because that would mean too many questions with uncertain answers. I wasn't sure whether I could let myself feel comfortable with him, could let myself touch him. I read too much into every glance he gave me. I scooted my chair next to his, then worried I was sitting too close.

He was centered on Josh, making sure Josh was getting what he needed, taking care of him in every way. But every now and then, he flicked his gaze over to me and gave me a small, private smile. Or he let his fingers run across the back of my hand. Or he pressed his ankle against mine under the table.

I was in over my head and I knew it, and probably everyone near us could see it, plain on my face, in the way I held myself. I wanted *this*—what Josh and Nicky had, this ease between the two of them. This safety in the presence of the other. And I didn't know how to be the kind of person who reached out for that anymore. I didn't know how to be someone who could offer that in turn.

I switched my focus back to Nick and Joshua, his chubby fingers all covered in ketchup. I told myself to stop thinking, to be present. Josh was talking again, rambling on and on about—I thought, when I could make out the words—a book with puppies in it. And everything the puppies did. And the sounds they made. And something about pigs, but maybe I got that mixed up. It was hard to tell, because he zipped from one subject to the next without pause or thought, a true stream of consciousness.

"Chew with your mouth closed," Nick reminded him, leaning over to wipe crumbs away. "Wait until you swallow before you talk."

Josh gave him what was nearly a toddler eye roll, and I laughed. It *was* pretty gross. But I found myself fascinated by Josh. I was already exhausted, but there was something almost energizing about being with him too.

Every time I'd ever heard anyone talk about kids, they'd used the word *innocence*. And there was definitely an innocence to Josh. A complete unawareness of exactly how the world worked, of all the things that could go wrong. His world, instead, was this moment, and maybe the next few, and that was all. His world was his dad sitting next to him and, for right now, me. But I wasn't sure if it was the innocence of his childhood that struck me and drew me to him. Maybe it was the possibility in him. Not the possibility in any kid, but in *him*, in Joshua.

It was stupid of me, but I hadn't realized kids had such personalities already. I'd thought they were kind of . . . half-formed blobs of people. But Josh was a person. He had ideas and wants and things he liked, and things he found funny, and things that made him glare at Nick. When he wasn't looking adoringly at Nick, that is, because Josh had people he loved too. And he was, obviously and deeply, loved in return. The idea that all of that was already there, that this person had so much possible time stretching out in front of him, that he could make of it whatever he pleased, was wonderful to me. Frightening, because I already liked him, and I knew what life could do to a person. But wonderful. Endless possibilities for this personality, for this person.

And when I was wrapped up in Josh and Nick, when my focus went back to them, I couldn't take it away again. So I didn't care, after all, what anyone else thought of us. It didn't matter.

By the time we left the restaurant, it was quickly heading toward afternoon.

"I promised him time at the park," Nick said as we walked to the car. "But you don't have to come." He glanced down at Josh, smiling fondly at him. "I know he's wearing."

I hesitated, then asked, "Would you mind? I'd like to." It was true. Josh was a lot, especially since I wasn't used to kids. But I liked being with him. And I really liked being with Nicky.

Nicky grinned at me. "Not at all. There's a place near my house. He'll be totally done afterward, so it's probably a good idea."

The park, I saw when we got there, was small, but it had everything a kid could want—grassy spaces, a sandbox, swings, and a slide. We had to park down the street, and Josh bounced along beside us excitedly as we walked, his hand firmly wrapped in Nick's.

Josh headed straight for the swings as soon as Nick let go of his hand, and Nick himself went to push him for a while. I sat on a bench and watched them. It should have been boring, but it wasn't. I liked seeing them together. I honestly hadn't had any idea of how I'd feel, seeing Nick with his kid. With a kid who wasn't . . . who didn't have anything to do with me. Who belonged to Nick and another person, a woman I'd never met and had barely heard about. It had been such a surprise when he'd told me, it had seemed almost too large to take in. To understand what it meant, in all those different ways. To him and to me. I'd actually tried not to think about it too much. But the night before it had hit me—it was Nicky, the man I'd basically fucked in an alley, the drummer with the huge, goofy smile and the brownest, sweetest, deepest eyes I'd ever seen, whose son I'd be meeting. I'd lain in bed last night and wondered if it would make him a different person in my eyes.

It didn't. And it did, at the same time. He was different. But not in a way I didn't recognize. It was as if he was more of himself. When Josh said something and they bantered back and forth, I could see the humor and the happiness in every line of Nick's body. And when Josh laughed, Nicky laughed back, loud and long, his whole face and body given over to it. When he looked at Josh, whether it was to tell him something or check on him, whether he was glad or exasperated with the little boy, there was this tenderness underneath. This spark in his eyes. This well of emotions that all belonged to Nick. Love in a form I hadn't really thought to study before. I could have been jealous of it, and honestly, part of me was. No matter what I was or wasn't to Nick, no matter where we went from here, he would never look at me in quite that way. But, mostly, I thought Josh was lucky.

After a little bit, Josh decided he was done swinging, and that he should go play in the sand. Nick had brought a small pail filled with toys—plastic trucks and cars, a plastic horse with its tail missing and,

I was surprised but pleased to see, a Barbie. He handed this treasure trove over, and Josh went off to play—dutifully staying where we could see him—and Nick sat down next to me.

"They tell you kids are exhausting," he said, a smile still picking at the corners of his mouth. "But I didn't really think I'd be tired all the time, when I'm with him. He wears me out. He's like a ball of fire."

"He's not what I expected," I blurted out.

Nick turned slightly toward me. Both of us were still keeping most of our attention on Josh, but Nick raised his eyebrow. "What did you expect?"

I tried to think about it, put it into words, but I couldn't. "I don't know. Nothing, really. Like . . . I couldn't imagine what he'd be like at all. I didn't expect . . ." I gestured in Josh's direction. "So much."

Nick laughed and nodded. "Yeah. He's pretty awesome though, right?" He said it easily, without any vanity. Just a quiet kind of pride in his kid.

"Yeah. He is." I wasn't . . . saying it just to say it, to agree with him. I didn't think I was magically cured of my confusion about kids, or that I wanted to run off and have a bunch of my own, and I thought if I spent more than a day with Josh, I might drop dead, because there was no way I was keeping up with that energy level. But he *was* awesome. Maybe, simply, because in a lot of ways he reminded me of Nick.

"I'm always afraid I'm going to screw up," Nick said, softer, his voice low, and I wasn't sure if he wanted me to hear the words, or respond to them.

The question startled me, because it so mirrored the worries that had been running through my own mind. About screwing up with Josh. About screwing up—again—with Nick. "Why? I mean, in what way?"

He looked at me, and our eyes met, and then he pulled his gaze away, back out over the park and the scruffy grass and the sand, to Josh. "I don't know. In any way, I guess. Like I wasn't always there, every day, so I didn't learn everything as I went, you know? And I'm still not with him all the time, so he . . . grows super fast, and he learns stuff, and then when I see him, I have to keep catching up. What if I'm not catching up fast enough? What if I make a mistake?" He shrugged. "I don't know. It's all vague. He's so . . ." He flicked his hand, but he didn't finish the sentence.

That did sound awkward, to say the least. But I figured there were probably lots of families where one parent or the other was away, for work or some other reason. Maybe not Nick's reason, but I bet it happened. It didn't make it inherently bad. "That's probably more common than you think. And it doesn't mean you're actually going to mess anything—him—up."

"No, but . . ." He frowned, scrunching his eyebrows together. "I'm not trying to whine about it. He wasn't . . . he wasn't a conscious decision, but I would never change it. I'm really grateful he's here. I love being with him."

"I know." It was obvious. I didn't have a second of doubt about it, and I didn't think Joshua ever would, either. "And you're not whining."

He smiled, softly, and ducked his head, so I could only see his profile. "Sometimes I wonder if he'd be better with a normal dad. Someone who isn't . . . Someone with a normal job, someone who's . . . you know."

I shook my head. "I really don't."

"Someone who's respectable," he said all in a rush. "Someone who grew up and stopped having fantasies about being a rock star. His life's going to be so complicated already, because his mother and I aren't together. I wonder if he'd be better with something more solid."

I pulled in a sharp breath. I wasn't sure why, but it hurt to hear him say that. I ached for him, but it also made me hurt for his band, and for Escaping Indigo. And for me.

"Don't say that." My voice came out harder and sharper than I'd meant it to. "First, he isn't going to be . . ." I made a vague gesture. "Damaged or something because his parents aren't together. You're making it work, you both love him, so it's fine." I waited until he nodded before I continued. "Second, you are completely respectable. And you're not having fantasies—you worked hard and you did it. You made it. You got to this point, you *are* a rock star. It's not a pipe dream. It's reality. And what you do . . ." I was working myself up, my voice getting louder, and I had to rein it back under my control. "You make people happy with your music. You make them feel something, something important. You create something incredible and beautiful.

Don't you think that's more important than being normal, than being like everyone else? For you? Maybe for Josh too?"

His eyes were wide, and he was flushed, from his cheekbones down to his neck. "I'm just the drummer."

"Bullshit, you're just the drummer. Without you, the songs have no heartbeat."

For a second, he stared at me, his mouth open in an O. Then he laughed, hard enough that he collapsed forward and wrapped his arms around his middle. People turned to stare at us, he was so loud. Josh looked up, and I smiled and shook my head, pointing him back to his sandcastle.

"Sorry," Nicky said when he could talk again. "You looked so serious. Like it was a personal insult or something." He wiped at his eyes. He was still red, but not from embarrassment this time. His grin was so wide, it made my chest tighten, made my breath come short, the tiniest bit.

"I was. Kind of. I like your music, you know." I was almost mumbling now, embarrassed both by what I'd said and by how he'd reacted. And by how pleased I was at his laughter.

He swiveled around on the bench. "I know."

I sighed. "What I mean is . . . I think your job is respectable. And I think it makes you more interesting as a dad, not less. It means . . . Joshua's going to grow up thinking he can do whatever he wants, be whatever he wants. Isn't that better than not?"

He nodded. He was staring at my face, his gaze taking in my mouth, my eyes, searching for something, or studying me. "It is. Maybe. Hopefully." He reached out and touched the tips of his fingers to my arm. It was such a simple gesture, after the ways we'd touched in the past. After I'd literally had my hand down his boxers and around his dick the day before. We hadn't touched like that very often, though, and we hadn't talked about the night before yet, either. This touch was soft and intimate and it felt like it connected us in a subtle, important way. "Thank you."

I took a deep breath and nodded back. Josh yelled something to us, breaking the current of tension between us, and we got up and wandered over. We ended up sitting in the sand with him, letting him dictate stories to us with his toys. I hadn't ever thought I'd be a "get in the dirt and play with the kid" type of guy, but apparently I was. Apparently, if Josh turned his big puppy-dog brown eyes on me, so similar to Nick's, I was a goner.

"Don't let him bully you." Nick looked back and forth between me and Josh. "He knows exactly how to get what he wants."

I laughed but shook my head. "I want to." I scooted closer to Josh, who held up a car for me to use in the sand.

Nick and I spent another hour or so pretending we were kids again, building sandcastles and car tracks and whatever else Josh's limitless imagination could cook up. It didn't all make sense, and it flowed from one idea to another, so I was often strongly corrected by Josh when I assumed we were still in the same imaginary play game and he'd moved on. I liked it, though. I liked how he wasn't constrained by lines of thought. How his world and his mind were open.

He reminded me of Eric in that way. He reminded me of Eric a lot. Not so much when Eric was a baby—we'd been six years apart, which was enough for me to remember him as a little kid, but not a lot. It was more that Eric . . . had always been a kid to me. He'd always been someone I'd wanted, needed, to look after. He'd always, in some ways, been *my* kid—our dad had left when we were young, young enough that I could barely remember him, and it had been our mom, and Eric, and me. I'd always wanted to step into that role of protector and guide and caretaker for Eric. I'd always wanted to be there for him.

I just hadn't been very good at it.

The thought kept popping up while I watched Nick go back and forth between play mode and dad mode, while I watched him watch Josh like he'd never take his eyes off him. I tried to push it away, because it wasn't really fair, to me or to Nick. Our situations were completely different. Like Micah had always tried to tell me, Eric hadn't needed me to look after him. That wasn't why things had gone for him the way they had. But I'd never really seen Eric as grown-up, as independent. I couldn't help thinking that maybe if I'd tried harder, been there more, done more, taken better care of him, he'd still be alive. It was different for Micah, because as close as he'd been to Eric, Eric hadn't been his brother. I was supposed to be dependable. I had responsibilities to Eric, more than I did to anyone else. I should have been there, and I should have done better.

It was an idea that floated around in my head all afternoon. By the time we were ready to go, Josh was tired and getting whiny—although, not nearly as much as I'd expected from a two-year-old. I was sure he had his tantrums, little-kid moments, but while I'd been with him he was so happy all the time. We packed up the stuff, and Nick invited me back to his place for dinner. And then, somehow, I ended up carrying Josh back to Nick's car. Josh was sleepy enough that he laid his head on my shoulder, and he stayed there, a heavy, warm lump, his fingers curled into the fabric of my shirt, my palm against his back, until Nick took him to buckle him into his car seat.

Nick's house was big, and it was in a nice neighborhood. Rest in Peach had been doing really well over the last couple of years, and it showed in what they were able to afford. Nick caught me gazing around the huge entryway, the living room with its giant, cushy couches and vaulted ceilings, the kitchen I could see off to one side, the hint of gleaming granite countertops and stainless steel.

"It's crazy, right?" he asked me, that grin back on his face. He looked slightly uncertain, though. "I grew up in a shithole." He glanced down immediately, to see if Josh was close enough to hear his foul language, but Josh had already run off into the house.

I nodded. "Me too." I still didn't live anywhere nearly as good as this place. Not that Escaping Indigo didn't pay me well. I could have moved, probably. Out of my old neighborhood and into something nicer, something closer to the rest of the band. But I . . . hadn't.

Nick wandered into the kitchen, kicking off his shoes as he went, and I followed. Josh had disappeared into a corner of the living room that was packed with toys.

"Sometimes I'm like, yup, this is my house," Nick said over his shoulder. "And sometimes I can't believe this is actually where I live. Like, what karma did I have in my past life that I got this, you know?"

I joined him in the kitchen. He was standing at the island, his hands flat against the edge of the stone. I took him in with the place, the roughness of him, of his drumming clothes, against all those sleek, smooth, expensive surfaces. But he didn't not fit here. He actually fit really well. He was angular and fine-edged, and instead of making him appear small as a house like this would have done for me, it made Nick look shiny and perfect. It made him look like he was at home. Because, I reminded myself, he was.

Nick made Josh lie down for a nap for a while—I had no idea that kids had to have naps, but Josh, after a bit of initial whining, seemed pretty into the whole thing. And Nick was good too, cajoling him gently into settling down. He was so practiced at all of it, as if he'd been taking care of a toddler his whole life.

When he came back after getting Josh to sleep, Nick and I cooked together. He told me he'd do all of it himself, but I didn't want to sit there and do nothing. So we made a super-complicated lasagna, messing up more than we were successful, probably. It looked good when we got it in the oven, though. Cheesy and full of herbs, all the layers just so. Then Nick got me a drink and we sat at the island in his kitchen, waiting for Josh to wake up. All of it was so . . . domestic. So family-like. And so comfortable and easy. I could imagine myself slipping into this role, this spot. Being here, with the two of them, or having them at my place. It felt so good. So warm and welcoming, and there was a big part of me that wanted that.

But it was terrifying at the same time. Overwhelming and big and too much. There were so many ways and reasons for it to go so wrong.

After dinner, I offered to do the dishes. Nick argued that I was a guest, and I argued that he'd now fed me twice, and all I'd done was buy lunch for them this afternoon and help him lay out sheets of pasta. We ended up doing them together, me washing or stuffing things in the dishwasher, Nick drying, until Josh came back into the kitchen and told Nick in no uncertain terms that he wanted to drum now.

It was evening by then, and I should probably have been going. But Nick was grinning at me, and I couldn't help grinning back. I didn't want to leave quite yet.

"You want to drum too?" he asked, his voice playful and teasing.

I laughed and nodded, and the two of us dutifully followed Josh to a room at the back of the house. It was small, and soundproofed. Maybe it had started life as a bedroom or office, but now it was a drum room, with two kits set up in it, and a third stacked in a corner.

I closed the door behind us, and Nick started adjusting one of the kits for Josh, moving everything closer so he could reach to hit stuff.

He picked Josh up and Josh wiggled around on the seat, his hands going right for the sticks resting on the floor tom.

"Use these, buddy." Nick pulled a pair of shorter, bright-blue sticks out from a pile.

He reached for some noise-canceling headphones too, and handed me a pair. "He doesn't hold back," he warned me, and I laughed. Josh laughed too, wild and happy. Nick plopped a smaller pair of headphones on Josh's head. Then he stood behind Josh and let him go to town.

The headphones blocked out a lot of the sound, making the snare and toms thumpy and muffled, muting the sharp, cutting crash of the cymbals, but it didn't stop the noise completely. And it was basically a cacophony. Josh, being two, had zero sense of musicality or rhythm or anything that made listening to a bangy instrument non-painful. It was awful. But Nicky stood behind him with the biggest smile on his face, and watched him with absolute pride, and I couldn't help smiling back at both of them.

God, they were perfect. Ridiculously, impossibly perfect, and I could see myself falling in love with them. Falling in love with the love between them. It was as if, standing here, watching them, I *was* falling, like I had tipped right over the edge of a cliff and was rocketing to the ground. Like I couldn't get my breath fast enough, like everything in me had tensed for impact, and I wasn't sure if I wanted it to end or go on forever. I couldn't tell if it was a good feeling or something to be frightened of. Or both at once.

Josh paused, finally, and Nick clapped out a slow, easy rhythm of a few beats. Josh copied it pretty closely by banging away on the drums. They repeated that a few times, with Nick changing the rhythm slightly each time, and Josh copying him.

"All right, kiddo," Nicky said after the last time. He gently pried the drum sticks out of Josh's hands. "Probably time for you to start getting ready for bed."

Josh put up a fight, arguing and demanding to play more, but Nick shushed him and, when that didn't quite work, he talked over him, directing his words to me. "I'm gonna go put him to bed. It'll probably be a few minutes to get him to calm down and sleep. Do you want to wait for me? I'll be back in a bit."

I nodded. Nick scooped Josh up, told him to say good night to me—Josh paused in his wailing argument and said good night very seriously, and then started his demands back up again—and they disappeared down the hallway.

I wandered back out into the living room and sat on the couch. I wanted to lean my head against the overstuffed cushion, but a full day with Josh had worn me out, and I was afraid that if I did, I'd nod off.

Nick came back after about a half hour. He leaned over the back of the couch, so his face was next to mine, chin resting on his folded arms. He was close enough that I could feel the warmth of his skin, could smell the clean, fresh sweat scent of him. I didn't have to turn my head to see the tired, lazy smile on his lips.

"Hey." His voice was a soft, low blur of sound, rumbly and private. "Sorry that took so long. I shouldn't have let him wind himself up before bed. I lost track of time."

I shrugged. "It's fine." And it was. I hadn't minded sitting there. I hadn't tried to listen to Nick and Josh while Josh got ready for bed, but their mingled voices had drifted down the hall, the quiet sounds of bedtime—teeth brushing and story reading—just reaching me. It had been comforting in a way I hadn't thought of in a long time. That strange, familiar childhood warmth of family and being with people you loved. It reminded me of being on the tour bus, hearing the quiet, murmured conversations between people settling in for the night, the deep, long breaths of sleep, the snuffle-y swish of sheets against pajamas. Being close. It reminded me of my mom and Eric, of the way our house had been in the evenings, all of us together, even when the three of us, all introverts, were in our own bubbles.

"Is that how you teach someone to play drums?" I asked, because I'd wondered in a vague way while I was watching them and it was the first thing that came tumbling out of my mouth.

Nick shrugged too, his chin bouncing on his forearms. "Sort of? It's more complicated than that, but that's the heart of it. Copy stuff until you know how to do it, until it's all muscle memory, and then start playing with it."

I turned toward him a bit, so I could see him better. "I wouldn't know. I'm the least creative person ever."

He studied me for a moment, really intently, his expression serious. "I doubt that, Quinn."

I shook my head. He straightened, standing up, and held out his hand. "Come on. I'll show you."

I shook my head again, slower this time, unsure.

"Yeah." He nodded back instead, encouragingly. "It'll be fun. Come on."

He was smiling, but it was softer, more serious than the grin he usually wore. He looked like he wanted to prove something to me. Or to the two of us. And I couldn't say no again, although I was pretty sure I was going to embarrass myself.

I took Nicky's hand and let him pull me off the couch, and I followed him back into the drum room. He glanced back and forth between the two kits and brought me over to the larger—and in my mind, more intimidating—one. I'd never been intimidated by an instrument before. They were what I dealt with day in and day out—them, and the musicians who played them. One drum set was much like another to me, although I *did* know all the pieces, how all of them should go together, exactly how Ava wanted everything. But I didn't understand the different sounds wood or plastic shells made. I didn't know why Ava used one type of drum head for recording and another for live stuff. And I didn't know why Nick had three drum sets here. All I knew was that this one had more drums around it, and more cymbals, and it was bigger, the drums wider, than the kit he'd let Josh play.

"Hang on a sec." He dropped my hand and moved over to the kit, pushing stuff around an inch or two and fiddling with the throne. "Okay. Try that. You're not much shorter than me, so I don't know how much of a difference it'll make."

I walked over and sat on the seat, tentative. It was harder than I expected, to get myself behind the kit. I had to carefully squeeze my leg in front of the seat, to spin around and face the drums, because there was stuff in the way. Stands and pedals to get tangled up in, and the snare, right there, practically in my lap when I finally got settled.

Nick moved around me, continuing to push and pull things, frowning in concentration. He also pulled out some round, black pads, which he plopped on top of each of the drums. "For the sound," he explained. "I don't want to wake Josh back up." Then he stepped back and stared at me, taking me and the drum set in together. I was bizarrely self-conscious. Sitting behind Nick's kit made me feel inexperienced, naïve. Uncertain and a little bit off-balance.

"How does that feel?" he asked me after a second.

I raised my eyebrows at him. "I have honestly no idea."

He flashed me a smile, then walked to a pile of drumsticks on the floor. I'd thought maybe he'd have more of a place for those, like a box or a bag, but they were just . . . piled. He grabbed a pair that matched. They were somewhat worn, splinters coming off the ends, but when he put them in my hands, the part my palms gripped was smooth, silky almost. Worn soft by Nicky's fingers.

"Okay, so." He crouched to one side, almost under the high-hat, and took one of my hands in his. "You want to hold the stick near the end. Don't choke up on it. This is your fulcrum." He held up his own hand, and pressed his thumb to the middle of his pointer finger. On my own hand, my thumb pressed the stick into that spot on my finger. "Let your other fingers flop for a second." I did, and when I moved my wrist, pinching at the fulcrum he'd showed me, the stick moved up and down.

He reached out again and curled my fingers gently back around the stick. "Keep it loose. Don't grip too hard. Curl your pinky around the stick. It'll keep it from slipping. Wrist straight, or pretty straight. The back of your hand up to the sky." It was awkward. I hadn't ever realized there was so much to holding a stick. I figured you just grabbed it and held it however you liked. But when he'd gotten me adjusted, it was comfortable, and I could see how this would make every move after easier, more fluid.

He stopped, like he realized how into this he was getting. "Sorry." He quirked his mouth up in a half smile. "It's important. So you don't hurt yourself. But it probably doesn't matter right now."

I shook my head. His fingertips were still resting on my wrist, the touch light. I swallowed hard. This was all fun, I reminded myself. Everything we did. Yesterday and today and this, right now. Just fun, and I couldn't ruin it by saying any of the serious, sappy things running through my mind.

I wanted to, though.

I choked all those responses back and made a joke instead. "Now what, O Wise One?"

Nick laughed, and it broke the tension building between us. But he was serious as well, about the drumming. I could tell, even though he kept sending me those bright smiles, and I wanted to be serious about this too. For him.

He stepped back and stared at me, scrutinizing me, and I tried not to squirm. "Feet on the pedals. Press your high-hat down enough to keep it closed."

I followed his instructions. I was barefoot, my shoes at the door because I'd been afraid of what I might track onto his pristine white carpet. The metal under my foot was cool and grooved with the pedal's brand and number, rough and slick at the same time. I slid my foot up it until it was comfortable, then I pressed down. The high-hat shut with a crisp snap.

"Good. Now the bass. Don't press down. Just rest your foot there so you could if you wanted to."

I stepped on the bass pedal. The beater thumped softly against the drum head before I pulled back enough. I looked back at Nick. He was grabbing another foam pad, and he slipped it down the back of the bass drum, between the head and the beater.

"Almost forgot. Probably we can't play on the high-hat, either. That's okay." He gave a small shrug and pointed at the biggest floor tom. "We can use that. But for now put your sticks over the snare." He nodded when I was positioned correctly.

I was pretty sure I'd never felt more awkward than I did sitting there, legs splayed, hands held carefully in front of me so I didn't accidentally make a sound.

"'Kay. Now we play." Nick took a breath. I couldn't quite hear it, but I could tell how deep it was with the rise and fall of his chest. "Do 'one, two, three, four,' on the snare. Just tap. Right, left, right, left." He mimed the pattern with his hands on his thighs, almost like he'd done for Josh. But this pattern was much simpler. Only four beats, evenly spaced. Simpler than what he'd given a two-year-old. That was okay with me. Simple was good. Cautiously, not really sure what I was nervous about, but sure I *was* nervous, I copied him, tapping the tips of the sticks in the middle of the snare. Right, left, right, left.

"Good, okay. Now do it on the tom." He pointed at one of the middle toms. "Same pattern."

I did, and he had me go around the kit that way, hitting the four toms, and then, very gently, so the sound was slight, the crash, the ride, and the China cymbal he had set up. It was simple. Just a display of different sounds.

"Now go back to the snare and do it again."

I did.

"Now play it really hard."

I hesitated, then walloped the sticks down in the same rhythm. It was . . . fun. God, yes, it was fun. I couldn't hear it much, with the pad covering the drum. It was only a whumping sound. But it was good to feel all those muscles in my arms straining briefly with the exertion. Cathartic, even that small amount.

"Now soft." His voice went softer too, lower, more gravelly. I looked up, and our eyes caught for a split second. The gaze held, and then I turned my face back to the drums in front of me. There had been something dark and intense in his expression.

I played softly, like he'd asked. There was something about following his instructions, doing only as he said, that was soothing when everything about this was strange and new and uncomfortable.

"Now go around the kit like before." His voice was still low. He was walking toward me, one slow step at a time. He circled the kit so he could come up beside me. "It's only evenly spaced beats. You can play them wherever you like. On the drums or the cymbals. You can split them up in different groups. You can play soft or hard or in between." He gave a small laugh. "Don't play the cymbals loudly, though."

I swallowed and nodded. At first, I was too self-conscious to do anything more than move around the kit in a circle, four beats to each instrument, medium loud. It was as if every sound I made was a way of flinging some bit of me out into the space of the room. Like I was making *myself* loud. Like I was shouting through the drums, but I wasn't sure what I was saying, or if I wanted anyone to hear. But Nick didn't reprimand me for playing it safe. He didn't urge me to do more. He waited, and let me go around again, and again, until some of the uncertainty slipped away, and I actually listened to the sounds

I was making with the sticks. The sharp pings and sandy clashes of the cymbals. The brassy gong-like whoosh of the China, even when I only tapped it gently. The thumps of the drums themselves, snappy and rattly on the snare, and then deeper and deeper with each floor tom, even with the sound muffled, so I imagined I could feel the last one in my bones.

I stayed on the biggest floor tom for a while, playing those same beats, changing how hard I struck, listening for what sounded good. Then I went backward instead of continuing the same circle around. Then I hit the things I liked the best, the things that made the most pleasant sounds to my ears. I experimented. I played—not like playing an instrument, but like a kid playing, exploring. I got lost in it for a handful of minutes.

"See," Nicky said when I finally slowed to a stop. "You made something that was your own, there. If you didn't have any creativity in you, you wouldn't have been able to do that."

"It was just noise," I said, coming back down off the odd high of having made such a racket. I let my hands, still closed around the sticks, drop to my lap.

Nick shrugged. He'd moved so he was standing almost behind me, but I could still see him out of the corner of my eye. "That's really all music is. Noise in a pattern, fitting with other patterns."

I couldn't argue that. And, more than that, I didn't want to. I wanted him to be right. I didn't think I was ever going to be artistic in any way, not like he was, or Bellamy, or Tuck or Ava or anyone in Rest in Peach. But what I'd done had been . . . fun, and freeing in a way I hadn't quite imagined. I didn't really think music was quite so simple. But part of me wanted him to be a little bit right.

He stepped fully behind me, and bent so he could cover my hands with his. His chest pressed against my back, and I could feel him breathing on my neck. Without saying anything, he picked up my hands, and I let him guide me. The tempo was slower this time, so he could move us both. But he danced us around the kit, my hands moving over the drums and cymbals wherever he put them, bending my elbows to hit here, or there, to make this sound, or this one. He didn't change the dynamics too much—I doubted he could, playing like this, with me in the way—but he broke those evenly spaced beats up into different chunks, twos and threes and eights and then back to three, then five, so the sound was always unexpected—syncopated and strange and melodic in the most incredible way. And there were patterns in it. Patterns that were hard to pick out, patterns that were nearly invisible if you weren't searching for them. Patterns I couldn't always decipher. But he had all those movements ingrained in his muscles, and all he had to do was call them up.

When we stopped this time, he let my hands go, but didn't pull away from me. I listened to him breathe, the rough sound of his breath a perfect counterpoint to the last lingering ring of the cymbals we'd hit together. I was breathing quickly too, although none of it had been a workout. None of it had been difficult. But there had been that catharsis again, and the sense of . . . opening myself up to something vast. And Nicky had gone with me that last time, and it had made it so incredibly good. I didn't think what we'd done counted as making music together, since I hadn't been in charge of the noises. But it felt like it, in a way. It felt like we'd made something together, and released it, and now it was a thing, floating in the air between us on those last notes.

I didn't want this, whatever was between us, to end this time. It hit me like a crack of lightning. Like the sharp sound of the stick against the snare. The snap and then the lingering echo, this feeling that chased all the way through me. I had agreed to only right now, only these weeks together, but I didn't want only that. I didn't think I was good for more than that, not truly. But this wouldn't be enough, and I had probably known that, honestly, from the start.

I leaned back, enough to press against Nicky. And he moved forward the same amount, holding me, pushing back, giving me something to lean on. I dropped the sticks. Just opened my hands and let them go, and they clattered to the floor, bouncing off the metal legs of the snare stand, the high-hat pedal. When I turned around, Nicky was already reaching down to cup my face, his thumbs sliding over my cheekbones, his fingers brushing behind my ears, into my hair.

He dipped his head and pressed his mouth to mine. The kiss was a lot like the ones we'd had the night before. A rush of want, a heady need, and gentleness, tenderness, a certain care, like we both wanted to be easy with each other. But there was something deeper in it too, something that seemed to connect us further, at least to me. Maybe it was because it had been a long day and we were both tired, or maybe it was because Nicky had just shown me a piece of myself I hadn't known existed. Maybe it was because Nicky was feeling the same things I was, right at that moment. Either way, this kiss was different. More serious. More demanding. More all-encompassing.

I stood up, stumbling to get myself untangled from the kit and the throne, and moved Nick back. He went, until he bumped up against a wall, and it was like déjà vu. But then he laughed against my mouth, so I could feel the puff of his breath and the curl of his smile, and pulled away enough that he could talk.

"Can we make it to a bed this time?" He was standing on his toes, which made no sense, because it meant he had to lean down more than usual to kiss me. But when he spoke, he bounced up on them again, like there was an energy or excitement in him he couldn't control. "I really . . . I liked what we did last night in the alley. A lot. But I want . . ." He closed his eyes and dropped his forehead to rest against mine, and took a steadying breath. "I want it to be like it was before. I want to see . . ."

I nodded. I knew what he meant, and wanted that too, even if I couldn't put it into words. I wanted to know if we still fit in that perfect, oddly familiar way we had the one time we'd come together in bed before. I wanted to know if he still felt right when he was stretched under me, or when he was on top of me, leaning over me. I wanted to know if we were still good, if we still worked, when we were slow and careful, and not rushed and desperate.

My hands were around his wrists, and I tugged them down and took a step back. I didn't let go of him, though. I didn't want to do that. "Lead the way."

He brought me to the other side of the house, and I was grateful we were as far from Josh as we could get. Obviously, lots of people had sex while their kids slept down the hall. But maybe I wasn't used to the idea, because it made me pretty uncomfortable. When we got into the bedroom, Nick locked the door behind us. He laughed when he saw my raised eyebrows.

"He knows to knock, or call out, if he needs me. But I don't want him walking in on us. He doesn't need to see that." He poked the tip of his tongue out. "Too many questions."

It broke some of my nervousness, washed it away, and I laughed.

"Come here." I caught at his hands again, pulled him toward me, and he pushed, so we ended up tumbling onto the bed. "How do you want me?" I asked, breathless and suddenly finding everything less funny and more . . . intense. His weight on me was wonderful, heavy and strong. He was so warm, the heat of him seeping into me. I imagined I could feel the pounding of his heart pressed to mine.

He raised himself up onto his elbows and kissed me again. "Like last time," he said when he moved away. "Last time we were in an actual bed."

I nodded, and sat up enough that he could reach down and take my shirt off.

It wasn't at all like last time, really—or the last time before the alley. That time, we'd been flirting endlessly for weeks, with only a few stolen kisses between us. That time, when we'd finally gotten a moment to ourselves, we'd rushed into it, desperate just to come together. It had been dark, the moon new, only the hint of lights shining in through the windows, and I hadn't been able to see him very much. We'd fumbled our way through it, and it had been perfect, and I wouldn't have ever wanted to change it. But this time was *different*.

I could see him, for starters. He'd turned on a bedside table lamp, and it cast a low, warm glow that lit up his skin and made his eyes shine. I was glad for it, because he was beautiful and I wanted to stare at him forever. But it seemed to make us nervous too. Instead of undressing each other, we mostly peeled our own clothes off in a clumsy dance: Nicky getting caught in the wide arm holes of his tank top, which should be impossible; me hopping on one foot to shake my jeans off. When we were finally naked, we just stood there beside the bed, facing each other. Taking each other in.

He laughed, maybe at the absurdity of us standing there, naked and nervous, and it was infectious. I laughed with him, while I kept staring at him.

He really was gorgeous. Angular and sharp, all joints and bone. His stomach was flat and his legs were long and lean, corded with muscle. I wanted to run my hand up the back of his thigh and feel that, the build of him, the strength there. His laughter slowed, and he tilted his chin up like he knew what I was thinking.

I wasn't gorgeous or beautiful like Nick. I was just this side of hairy, and I didn't bother to keep it much in check or try to make it look good. It swirled around my nipples and across my pecs, then petered out, only to come back in force in the thick path that led to my groin. My skin wasn't smooth like his, either. I'd had acne as a kid, and I had scars here and there to prove it, across my cheeks and along my shoulders. I was tan in odd places, from where I wore a tank top or a T-shirt, bands of different-colored skin, freckled and spotted, dancing down my arms and my torso. And I was big. Big all over, except in height, to the slightness of Nicky. Wider muscles, larger bones. More strength maybe, but maybe not, too.

The way Nicky was watching me, though, made me feel more comfortable about all of that, despite how nervous I still was. He was staring at my chest and licking his lips, which should be laughable, and it was. It made me smile so wide. But it lit a fire inside me too, right under my breast bone. This hot spark of need and desire, traveling through my bloodstream, setting me alight. It made me want to do wicked things to him.

He raised his eyes to mine, and that was enough of a signal for me. I stepped forward and wrapped my arms around him, and he leaned on me, giving me his weight, like he'd taken mine when I was sitting at the drum set before. I walked us backward until we hit the bed again. The climb onto it was awkward this time, especially for me, going backward, and then we had to scoot our way up so we weren't hanging off the edge, but it didn't matter. If we were ungainly, we didn't care anymore. I was too lost in him, and he didn't take his eyes off of me.

It was better that way, to not care. Not care how we got to the bed or how clumsy we were doing it. Better not to think about what this meant, what it meant when I added it to last night.

I leaned back on his pillows. They smelled like him, like salt and the shampoo he used, something cucumber. It made it seem as if I were surrounded by him on all sides. He knelt over me, palms on either side of my head, and bent forward to kiss me. I reached up and cupped the back of his neck, pushed my fingers into his hair, teased my pinky down his nape. With my other hand, I gave in to my temptation from before and slid it between his legs to grasp his thigh. I ran it up, starting at his knee, brushing the tips of my fingers over the tender skin there, then moving higher. Rubbing my palm over smooth skin and the odd crisp-softness of his hair, letting my fingers drift around his leg as I drifted my hand up. Touching, so carefully, so lightly, that delicate stretch of muscle on the inside of his thigh. Edging my thumb into the crease where his leg met his groin.

He shivered, almost violently, the movement shaking his whole body, and pulled his mouth away from mine. "God, Quinn. What are you doing to me?"

His voice was breathy and harsh, but there was a smile behind it, a hint of humor.

I looked up at him and smiled back. I wanted to say something, maybe something sweet and cheesy. But instead his slight movement made my arm rise that last inch, so my wrist touched his balls, and he moaned and jerked forward, rubbing himself against me.

I'd never had anyone hump my arm before. It was . . . weird. Not my first choice for sexual activities, for sure. But there was something incredibly hot about him doing it, about making him so desperate for friction that he'd grab at whatever was there.

But I couldn't resist laughing, and he joined me, collapsing into giggles on my chest, his ass still sticking up in the air, my arm between us.

"Don't laugh at me," he whined, but he laughed more himself. "I fucking need something."

I kissed my way up his shoulder, along his neck. "I know. Come here." I moved my hand from between us and tugged at his hips, urging him to walk forward on his knees. He did until his knees were almost at my shoulders, and I could prop my head up on a pillow and reach forward to take him in my mouth.

This was entirely new. He'd sucked me the first time we'd been together, but we'd been too desperate to move on to other things to wait for me to return the favor. But *favor* wasn't the right word, because I loved doing this. Not always. Sometimes it was uncomfortable, or didn't feel right, or I wanted someone to pay attention to my body instead. But it was good with Nicky. Better than good, and I wanted it. The sounds he made, the moans and the sharp gasps of his breath, the way he rocked so carefully forward, pushing the tiniest bit into my mouth, gentle with me, while his legs trembled at the effort, made me want to keep doing this for as long as possible. I wanted to hear every noise, I wanted to feel every twitch of his body. I wanted to take everything he could give me.

I wanted to explore other places too, though. I pulled off, the sound as he slipped out of my mouth obscene enough to make me pause, eyes closed, and thrust my own hips up into thin air. When I opened my eyes, all I could see was Nicky, spread above me, his hands around the headboard, arms locked tight to brace himself. His eyes were closed, squeezed shut, and his mouth was open. He dropped his head down and let loose a harsh cry.

"Please, fuck. Please, Quinn."

I took his cock in my hand and rubbed my palm along it, holding it carefully out of the way. Then I urged him to lower down, so I could lick at the soft, sensitive skin behind his balls. And then farther back, to that crinkled opening. He moved as I did, short jerks of his hips, like he couldn't hold himself still. I let go of his cock and raised my hands to his hips, urging him on or asking him to stay still, I couldn't quite tell. Then I went to town, lapping at him with my tongue, pressing my nose against his taint, getting as close as I possibly could, touching him and licking at him until he shouted.

"Shush," I said, moving away enough to talk. "Gotta be quiet." Then I went back to what I was doing.

I wasn't practiced at this. I'd only done it for a few people. Like sucking cock, sometimes I'd liked it, and sometimes I hadn't. It had, I was pretty sure, way more to do with the person I was with than it did with the actual act. But I liked this with Nicky. He tasted . . . like Nick. Bitter and salty sweet, and his skin was so soft and tender against my mouth. And the way he moved over me, the way he seemed to lose himself, rubbing himself against me, pressing almost too close, too hard, before he remembered and gentled his movements, reining himself in so he wasn't too rough with me, was insanely hot. I did that to him. I made him lose his mind. I made him lose control.

I kissed my way back up, then rolled us so he was lying underneath me. "Lube?" I asked. And then I realized we hadn't talked about how we'd do this. I'd fucked him last time, but I was flexible. I didn't care what went where, or if we didn't do the whole insert tab A into slot B thing at all. I just wanted him, I wanted him to feel good, and I wanted to feel that way too.

But Nick was already twisting us back, trying to reach over me for the drawer of his bedside table. "In there." He waved his hand through the air. "There's stuff."

I turned over instead, and opened the drawer myself. There was *a lot* of stuff. "Holy shit." There was a box of condoms, and lube— the really high-end stuff I knew would be super silky on my fingers. I guess you could afford that when you were a rock star. I grabbed both items, but I couldn't turn away from what else was in the drawer. Toys. Maybe five or six. All really . . . nice? Could some sex toys be nicer than others? Classy? I had to admit I wasn't exactly an expert. I assumed they were still made of silicon, like your average, run-of-the-mill dildo, but they looked *better* than that somehow. There were a few different sizes, as well as a prostate massager and . . . "Are those sounds?" Holy fuck. Holy fuck. I was in over my head. They were in a box, but the cover was clear, and I could see them, all shiny, the metal bright, nestled in the velvet lining. I couldn't be positive, because I'd never actually seen any in real life, but I didn't think they could be anything else.

I glanced back to see Nick stretch and shrug, the movements casual, but a flush rose up his chest. "I wanted to see how they felt."

I shut the drawer, rolled onto my back, and dropped the lube and condoms on the bed beside me. "And? How were they?"

His lips curled up at the corners, sultry and sinful and gorgeous. "Fantastic." Then he leaned forward and brushed a sweet, nearly chaste kiss over my lips. "We can play with anything you want. But right now, I just want you, okay?"

I nodded. I wanted that too.

We hurried more after that. He straddled me again, but faced the other way so he could put the condom on me, while I slicked my fingers and pressed them inside him. He was quick, and he didn't let me touch him for very long before he was swinging back around to face me, rubbing some of the lube over my cock, and settling me at the entrance to his body.

"Ready?"

I laughed, but the sound was strained. "Aren't I supposed to be asking you that?"

He blinked and smiled. "It goes both ways."

I nodded. "Yeah. When you are."

He slid down onto me, and I had to close my eyes because it was so good. Heat and slick and the tightness of him around me, and knowing it was *Nicky*—Nicky, who I hadn't really ever expected to see again. Nicky, who I'd wanted all this time, but hadn't let myself want because I'd thought this part of my life, that part of my past, was dead.

It took us a minute to find the right rhythm. I thrust up too fast, too eager, and he grunted and tried to grind down, and everything was way too tight for a second, and awkward. I thought, for one panicked moment, that maybe that night a year ago really had been magic, and we actually weren't so good at this. But then he shifted, moving his knees closer around me, and I held his hip with one hand and ran the other over his chest, down his stomach, soothing, and everything clicked into place.

And after that . . . well, I never really thought of sex as perfect, because it was such a *human* thing, and the imperfections were what made it good. But this came about as close to perfect as I could remember. For those minutes while we moved together, everything made sense. Everything was okay, and this was where I belonged.

I came first. I couldn't help it. I'd let my hand drift down to Nicky's cock, and we were stroking him together, and he had his head tossed back and his eyes closed, his teeth buried in his lower lip. Then he shuddered when I hit the right angle inside him, and his head fell forward, his eyes snapping open, so he was staring directly at me. And that was all I could stand, all I could take. He was so beautiful and we were so connected and it was *immense*, heady and powerful. I came in a rush, thrusting up into him.

He kept moving until I was done, and then he inched forward, so I slipped out of him. He soothed me this time, running his hand along my collarbone, touching my jaw. When I came back to myself enough, he took my hand and guided it behind him, and I pressed two fingers into him. He was soft there, and I was careful, but I wanted him to feel everything, I wanted it to be good for him. I moved my fingers inside him while he stroked himself, and it didn't take too long before he came all over my chest.

He collapsed forward onto me, flinging an arm across my chest, and I held him to me. Nicky was the type of person who'd go right to sleep and wake up stuck to me, and in that moment I almost didn't care how gross that would be in a few hours. I dipped my finger into the come on my chest and licked it, and Nicky blinked and let out a guttural moan.

"Fuck, Quinn."

I laughed, tired, and gave him a gentle shove to move him off me. "Where's the bathroom?"

He pointed vaguely toward one of the doors in the room, and I found the bathroom and a damp cloth, and came back to wash us off. Then I climbed into bed beside him, and he did the limpet thing again, wrapping himself around me and squishing up next to me as close as he could get, so all the bits of our skin that could touch, were touching. I liked it.

The day was a blur in my mind, a whirlwind of activity, of Nick, and Josh, of the two bands, of everywhere we'd gone. And of this. The quiet at the end of it. The ease. The togetherness. The way being tired felt so rightfully good. Like all my joints were melting into the mattress and into Nicky, and I could stay right here forever, and not think about the studio, or the past, or Eric, or what I could have done better. For a little while, there was only this.

# chapter eight

X

When I woke up the next morning, Nicky was already out of bed. I lay still, letting myself wake up some more, taking in my surroundings. The lamp had been on last night, but I hadn't bothered to look around the room very much. I'd had other things on my mind. But now I had some time, and I could.

The room's color scheme wasn't white like the rest of the house. The walls were painted a pale blue, except for the wall behind the bed, which was a deep azure. The sheets I was lying on matched, and they were ridiculously soft and silky. Nick never seemed like someone who had a lot of money. He wore down-to-earth clothes, and he didn't drive a fancy car. But it came out in odd spots in his house—in his sleek sheets, in his pricy lube. I liked that he indulged himself where he wanted, that he liked to be comfortable.

The room was mostly empty, except for a chair in the corner, which had about a billion T-shirts and pairs of jeans slung over the arms and back. There were four or five pairs of different-colored high-top sneakers underneath it. And there was a keyboard on a stand in the corner. I didn't know if it was his. I'd never seen Nick play anything but drums.

I sat up and bent over the edge of the bed, searching for my clothes. Should I shower? Or would that be presuming too much? I could wait until I got back to the studio, but what if I wasn't going back right away? I shook my head at myself. I was being stupid. Nick probably wanted some time with his kid. We'd had our time together yesterday and last night, and I should give them some space. I should probably give myself some space too.

I grabbed my clothes. Then I made a quick trip to the bathroom, rinsed my mouth with the mouthwash on the counter, and combed my fingers through my hair. It wouldn't lie flat. It was long enough that it was starting to go wavy, and I had to tug at it to get it to go where I wanted.

When I stepped out of the bedroom and into the hall, I could hear voices. I paused, listening. Nick's voice was a low, amused rumble. Joshua's was higher, more excited, rising and falling like he couldn't contain all his energy. They laughed together, and something warm and sweet expanded in my chest. They sounded perfect together. Domestic bliss.

I couldn't remember Eric laughing. He'd had a very dry sense of humor, always making those sharp remarks that had you keeled over with laughter, surprised by how quick and wry he was. He would smile with you. A quirk of his mouth at one side that told you he was glad you were pleased. But he hadn't laughed much himself. Not because he was unhappy, but because he was quiet. He was always tucked away inside himself.

But I should be able to remember his laugh. I should be able to picture him with his head tossed back, his eyes lit with happiness. That shouldn't have been something I forgot. I should have spent more time with him in those last years. I should have been around more. Maybe then, memories wouldn't be slipping away from me in bits and pieces. It was just . . . I'd always figured I'd have more time. That there would be this . . . mystical moment in the future when things were settled and neither one of us was scrambling to get things done for our respective careers. I'd always told myself, in the back of my mind, that there would be more time. But there hadn't been. That moment had never come.

I shook myself, berating myself for getting lost in my own head. Sex did that sometimes. Seemed to open me up and make me vulnerable, where I usually kept such a tight rein on everything. This wasn't the time for it, though.

I walked through the living room and to the kitchen. But I stopped short outside the door. I wasn't sure if I should interrupt Nick and Josh. They seemed to be involved in a conversation, Nick answering things very seriously. I liked that he didn't use baby talk. He treated Josh like he was a small person, not an idiot. I couldn't stand outside the door and listen to them either, though, so I moved around the corner that had been concealing me and stepped into the kitchen.

Nick saw me right away, and he smiled like I'd brought the sun into the room. It made that warmth in my chest expand about a thousand fold, and I grinned back, probably looking loopy and overly happy, but I didn't care. He was standing behind the island, Josh in a high chair on the other side, and Nick waved me to the space beside Josh.

"If you don't mind," he added. "You can pull the stool away. He gets messy."

I shook my head and slid into the seat. "I don't mind."

"Good." He pushed himself up on the edge of the counter with his hands, leaning forward to brush a kiss over my lips. I hadn't expected it, really. Not in front of Josh. Maybe not at all. I didn't know if he'd want to, if that was . . . what we were doing. But I couldn't deny that it was nice. That it made me feel safe and cared for.

I turned and found Josh staring up at me. He had a little bit of maple syrup on his cheek, but otherwise, he was pretty clean for a two-year-old who was diving into breakfast.

"Hi, buddy."

"Hi." He turned back to his pancakes, apparently completely unconcerned with his dad's friend still being here in the morning. I couldn't decide if that was a good thing or not.

"We're having pancakes," Nick said, drawing my attention back to him. "Can you stay? I have to drop Josh off at his mom's after, but . . . we could have breakfast together?"

He sounded so hopeful. Like he thought there was any chance I was going to say no. I nodded. "I'd like that."

"Look," Josh demanded, earlier shyness forgotten in his eagerness to show me . . . something. He pointed at his plate, at the silver dollar pancakes Nick had made for him. "You put them in the stuff."

"The syrup?" Were you supposed to question what kids meant? Or were you supposed to go with it and pretend you understood?

"No, the stuff!" He pointed again, and I nodded, very serious.

"Is that so?"

"He means the butter," Nick explained, turning away from the stove. "He's an addict."

"Oh." I turned back to Josh and gave him a careful poke in the side, making him squirm and giggle. "Should we butter your paws, like a cat, so you always come home?"

It wouldn't make any sense to him—it didn't make any sense at all; I was nervous about talking to him and I was basically making stuff up on the fly—but he seemed to get the teasing tone, and he giggled that high, sweet, effortless little-kid giggle. I found myself laughing with him, and teasing him more, tickling him, avoiding his sticky hands.

I looked up and found Nick watching us, a happy, bemused expression on his face. Like he was glad we were okay together, but like we were also a puzzle he was trying to decipher.

"Do you want kids?" he asked, and I went from giddy and floating to feet on the ground in a single second.

"I don't know." I looked down at the counter, ran my finger over a line in the granite. "I never really thought about it, you know?" I glanced up, and he nodded. I supposed that was almost answer enough. I was over thirty. If I'd wanted kids, the urge probably should have popped up by now, shouldn't it have?

"Yeah, I get that."

"I always thought of . . . Eric was younger than me by a lot, and our dad was gone, and I always . . . My mom used to tell me I had to be a role model for him. That I had to be responsible. That's how I thought of him. As my responsibility."

Nick smiled. "That's what having a kid is like. Like someone gave you one hell of a responsibility."

I swallowed, my throat suddenly too dry, and nodded. "I don't think I was very good at it, though."

Nick shrugged, like he was trying to make the question lighter, disperse it. He turned back to the pancakes, but although he mostly had his back to me, I could feel his attention on me, as if he were still watching me. "I kind of think that nobody's very good at it," he said over his shoulder. "It's like it's all . . ." He waved the spatula through the air. "All trial and error. I screwed up so much. Especially at first. It's like this constant panic while you try to figure everything out." He flipped a pancake over, and flipped another two onto a plate. "Every day I'm worried I'm messing something up. But eventually you realize you *can't* figure everything out."

I nodded, even though he couldn't see me. He let the last two pancakes cook for a second more, then scooped them onto another plate, turned around, and set both plates down on the counter, one in front of me. He slid onto a stool and picked up the syrup, and poured it over his pancakes in a long drizzle. I copied him when he passed me the bottle.

"I just keep telling myself that he comes first." He glanced over at his son, moved Josh's plate a half inch so Josh could reach more easily. "And if I do that, then I'm doing okay."

I nodded again, and stuffed a bite of pancake into my mouth so I wouldn't have to say anything. I didn't know what *to* say. He was right, and I hadn't truly expected anything different.

I looked over at Josh, who was now drawing patterns in his maple syrup with his finger. Had I ever put Eric first? Had I ever sacrificed any piece of my own happiness for his? I'd always tried to do my best for him—I'd always stuck up for him, talked to him, been there for him when we were growing up. But then I'd gotten the job with the band, and it had been the only thing in my life that had ever felt completely right, had ever felt like it was the perfect space for me. Like I fit, like I belonged. It wasn't what I'd imagined I'd be doing, but I was good at it, and I liked it a lot, and I'd left home in a second to go with Escaping Indigo. I hadn't asked Eric what he thought, if that would be okay. I hadn't asked him if he needed me around, if I should stay. I hadn't considered it at all. Because I'd wanted to go, so I'd left, and I'd left him behind. It was as simple as that.

I watched Josh play, without a single care in the world, and I watched Nick watch him. I didn't think Nick was wrong to go be a musician, to go on tour. It wasn't the same as it had been for me and Eric. Nick would always be there for Josh. There wasn't any doubt of that in my mind. He might be on the road, but he'd always come home to him. He'd always be there for him if he needed him.

I hadn't been there for Eric. I hadn't only gotten a new job, I'd gotten a whole new life. New friends, a new place in the world that was solely mine, a place where I could be myself without ever having to say a word, and I'd wanted to keep it that way. I'd wanted to protect it, keep it safe and secret. Protect it from what, I didn't know. The outside world, maybe. The past. Everything in my life that I hadn't chosen for myself. But in doing that, I'd shut Eric out. We'd gone down our separate paths, in a lot of ways. I'd made my choices. And he'd made his.

Nick wasn't ever going to shut Josh out. He was going to take on that responsibility because, whether he'd chosen it or not, it was what he wanted now. It was obvious that there wasn't any other option he'd take now. It was good that way. It was the best thing.

I told myself that just because Nick was doing it right, didn't mean I'd done it wrong. But I couldn't keep the thought out of my head.

We finished breakfast, and Nick dropped me off at the studio.

"I'm going to run him to his mother's," he said, before I got out of the car. "And then I'll meet you back here, okay?"

I nodded, and this time it was me who leaned over for a quick kiss. He tasted sweet from the maple syrup and pancakes we'd eaten earlier.

I turned around so I could see Josh. "Bye, kiddo. I liked hanging out with you."

He beamed up at me. He wasn't shy at all, not really. He was so . . . trusting. I could still feel the weight of him in my arms, from when I'd carried him to the car from the park the day before. I could smell the sleepy, little-kid warmth of his skin. I didn't know when I'd see him again. I didn't know if I *would* see him again. Maybe this thing with Nick would fizzle out like last time. Maybe we'd realize it couldn't work. Yesterday, I would have been fine, not knowing if I'd ever lay eyes on Josh again. But now, it did something to my heart. I knew, at least a little, that I was transposing Eric on Josh. It wasn't fair or right. And I knew Josh probably wouldn't notice if I never came around again, but I couldn't help wondering.

Josh waved at me, and I waved back, and that hot, bright sweet spot I'd been carrying around in my chest all morning squeezed down on itself, contracting and imploding, until all it felt like was hurt and worry. I opened the car door and practically leaped out, calling a goodbye over my shoulder. I walked up the driveway to the door we'd been using to get in and out of the studio, and I didn't look back to watch Nick drive away.

# chapter nine

X

the upper rooms of the house were quiet when I let myself in and climbed the stairs. Both bands were down in the studio already. I was half-glad for the space and silence, and half-wishing there was someone around to talk to.

I walked around the kitchen, but I'd already eaten, so it wasn't like I could kill time there. I stopped and stared at the two mostly empty coffee mugs on the island. Micah's and Bellamy's, probably. They seemed to have claimed those seats.

Micah had put his life back together without Eric. He hadn't filled in any of the holes Eric had left—he'd made space for other people, other choices, other things. I knew it hadn't been easy for him. I'd been there with him, trying to help him through the roughest spots as best I could. Got him a job, got him a way out of the home and city that were all tangled up in his memories of Eric. Encouraged him to be with Bellamy. I hadn't meant to step in where I didn't belong. I just . . . I liked the guy. And I'd wanted to make up for not being there when I should have been, for not helping him support my brother.

I knew I was being ridiculous. That the day and night I'd spent with Nicky and Josh had nothing at all to do with Eric. I needed to move on, keep that in the past, and make the present its own thing. But it was like I was . . . adrift. Like the past and present were all tangled: Eric and Nick and Josh, responsibilities, being there for someone.

I couldn't quite figure out what I was feeling. I was pretty sure I was . . . happy. Really happy, like this amazingly good thing had happened to me—because it had—and I couldn't quite contain all the awesomeness of it. But stepping back into the house and the normal daily routine I'd been getting used to made things seem slightly out of place. As if reality had shifted a half an inch to the left. Around me, the house was quiet, except for the very faint strains of music coming up the stairs, and I could almost imagine that I was invisible and separate. As if two sides of my life—the side before I'd met Nicky, before I'd slept with him again, and the side after, with everything that meant and everything that came with it—were crashing together. And they weren't quite clicking correctly in my mind.

I wandered toward my bedroom, down the hallway with all the musicians' photos on the walls. All that history. All those songs, soaked into the walls and the floorboards of this place. Other sounds, too, probably: laughter and fights and shouting. Discussions, compromises. Whispered words of love, probably, to people in the same room, to people on a telephone line. This place could tell stories.

I flopped down on my bed. Tuck's was neatly made, and I remembered that his girlfriend Lissa had been on her way up. She must have gotten here yesterday. It was probably better that I'd stayed with Nick. Maybe I'd sleep on the couch tonight. Not that we weren't used to pretty close quarters when we were on tour, but if I could give them space, we'd all be happier.

I closed my eyes and tried to breathe deeply, take a second to myself while I had it, to reconcile the day and night I'd had with all the days to come. I couldn't figure out why things felt so out of place in this moment. Maybe I was just confused. It would be fine.

Footsteps on the stairs cut off my train of thought. For a second, the music from down in the studio got louder as the hallway door opened. Then it clicked shut again, the music cutting off. I turned my head, but I didn't bother to get up. Nobody knew I was here, and now that someone *was* here to talk to, I wasn't sure if I wanted the company.

It turned out I didn't have a choice. Ava came down the hallway, a muffin on a napkin in one hand. She was obviously headed for her own room, but ours was right at the corner of the hall, so she couldn't help seeing my feet dangling off the edge of the bed. She paused, then stepped into the room.

"When did you get back?"

I shrugged. "Fifteen minutes ago, maybe."

She took a bite of her muffin and chewed while she contemplated me. "Did you have fun?"

I nodded against the pillow. "Yeah."

"That sounds honest as fuck." She took another step into the room.

"No, I did, I just . . . Why are you up here?"

She paused, tensing up, her shoulders rising defensively. Then she slumped and walked the rest of the way into the room so she could sit cross-legged on the end of the bed. She swiveled to face me and offered me half the muffin. I shook my head.

"Lissa's here." She picked at the muffin, breaking off a chunk and stuffing it in her mouth. "If I don't have to watch her and Tuck being all lovey on each other, better for me."

I'd suspected, for a while, that Ava might have a thing for Tuck. She hid it really well, though, so I'd always wondered if it was all in my head. But there had been something . . . a certain way she looked at him, a longing in her. She'd never admitted it though. Definitely not like this. But I wasn't surprised.

"Cara?" I asked, not sure exactly what I was going for.

She smiled. "I love Cara. And I don't want anyone but her. I know Tuck and I aren't ever going to . . . We're never going to have that. And I'm happy for him that he has Lissa. But . . . sometimes it still hurts." She waved her hand around. Muffin crumbs scattered, and she stopped abruptly and started picking them off the bedspread and dropping them into her napkin. "It's like I'm staring at a possibility I can see but I can't ever touch. I don't really want it anymore. But it still hurts."

I nodded. "That makes sense."

She cocked her head to the side and smiled again. "Cara's flying in this afternoon. She took a week off." She got this flushed glow to her when she talked about her girlfriend. Like just the thought of her lit Ava up from inside. I wanted to tell her she didn't have that glow when she talked about Tuck, but I knew the way she felt about him, the relationship they had, was older and different. And I understood, in a way, seeing your future diverge from what you imagined it would be, or what you wanted. The loss of that, even when you were happy with what you had.

"Tell me about Nicky?" she asked, nudging the side of my leg with her knee. It was a pretty bald attempt to change the subject. I wanted

ELI LANG

to humor her. I didn't know what to say about Nick and our night, though, about Josh and all the time the three of us had spent together.

"He's . . . such a dad." It was the first thing that tumbled out of my mouth.

She laughed. "Right? It was weird to see. He was always wild. He still is. But he went into, like, parent mode."

"Do you like kids? Is that something . . .?"

She shrugged and ate some more of the muffin. "I never really wanted any?" She didn't sound convinced. "I mean, it was what I was supposed to want, you know. Being a girl. It's like it's my job. If you tell someone you don't want kids, they jump down your throat about how you'll change your mind eventually, how everyone really does deep down. 'Give it time.'" She waved her hand—the hand without the muffin, this time—like she was flicking that all away. "It's bullshit. But . . ." She looked down at her lap. "I think Cara would be a great mom. And sometimes I think I'd like to see that." She raised her eyes up to mine, and a smile flickered across her mouth. "Being in love is weird. It makes your brain mush."

"Yeah." I stared down at my own hands. God, the things I'd done with them yesterday. I'd held Josh. I'd helped him spoon up dinner onto his plastic little kid utensils. I'd held drumsticks, made music for the first time ever, really, and I'd liked it. And then, later, I'd touched Nicky. I'd held his face in my palms, skated my fingers over every part of him. I'd been inside him.

"Hey," Ava said, softly, but with concern in her voice. I looked up and found her staring at me, her smile gone, her eyebrows pinched together. "You okay?"

I nodded quickly. "Yeah, yeah, I'm fine. I . . . I had a really good time yesterday. With Nick, and Josh. And then, uh, I had a really good time last night. It was . . ." God, if I said *good* again one more time. But I couldn't think of another way to describe how it had been. How right it had felt. How much I'd wanted it, and been so happy it had happened, even while it scared me. "But then this morning, all I can think about is all the ways this is going to go wrong. I mean, he's got a kid. I can't . . . I don't know . . ." I hadn't actually realized *that* was what I'd been worrying about, until I'd said it out loud. All those jagged edges of my thoughts suddenly made way more sense.

"Sounds like you ran out of endorphins." She touched my knee—a light pat, but a reassuring one. "It happens—it's normal, after sex, for your brain to go into overdrive. Or crash. Sex opens you up in a lot of ways." Fuck, she was blunt. I was blushing all over the place, but she was completely calm. She wasn't exactly meeting my eyes anymore, though. "As for him having a kid . . . That's a lot to take on, man. I don't mean it's a reason not to be with somebody. But it's probably good that you're thinking about it. Kids are so fragile. I mean, it seems like they are. I'd be afraid to fuck it up."

I hadn't told her what I was thinking about Eric, but her thoughts were an eerie echo of everything that had run through my mind this morning. What if I did fuck it up? What if I was diving into this headfirst, and by the time I realized I was in too deep, it was too painful to get out?

Ava was watching me, an uneasy expression on her face. "Why do I feel like I just said the completely wrong thing?"

"You didn't." I sat up and stole a bite of her muffin. "It was what I needed to hear." She didn't look convinced, and I sighed. "I just keep thinking . . . about Eric."

Her face did something between a frown and a pout and some vaguely guilty, uncomfortable expression. "Like, missing him?"

I wobbled my head back and forth, not a nod and not quite a shake. "Yeah. I always miss him. But . . ." I drew my hands back into my lap and squeezed my fingers together. "I've had a long time to . . . not get used to it." I would never, ever get used to it or over it. My life would never be the same. I would always, always be missing him. "I've had time to start moving on," I finished, softly. "I can't forever be . . . I need to move on. Micah moved on. Even my mom is still . . . going, seeing her friends, doing her job. I need to, too."

"So what are you thinking about him, then?" She kept her focus on her muffin, her fingers picking little bits off, as if she didn't want to spook me by meeting my eyes. Didn't want to put too much pressure on me.

"I think it's . . . this place, and the recording, and Nick. And Josh," I admitted. "I keep trying to measure how Nick takes care of Josh with how I took care of Eric." I didn't say anything about how I was measuring it against how I took care of the band. How they had needed me and now all of them had someone else to do that. Ava was trying to be kind, and it wasn't anything she needed to feel bad about.

She cocked her head to the side, and now she did look up at me. "What do you mean?"

I took a deep breath. "I mean, I should have been there for him, and I wasn't. I mean I should have tried harder to take care of him."

Pure pity crossed her face, but she smoothed over her features admirably quickly. "Quinn. Eric was an adult. He didn't need you to take care of him."

"Everyone needs someone to take care of them," I argued.

She nodded slowly. "Okay. Good point. But I mean, you weren't actually responsible for him." She shook her head. "No, that sounds wrong, and it's not what I mean at all." She tilted her head back and stared at the ceiling, before dropping her gaze back to me. "He was his own person. Everyone needs to figure out their own stuff. If he'd needed your help, if he'd realized that he did, he would have asked you."

It was almost exactly what Micah had been saying to me all along. But coming from Ava, it was somehow different. Hit me differently. I always brushed off what Micah was saying when he said stuff like that, because I always figured he was trying to absolve me or something. That he was trying to take away my guilt. I'd never quite convinced myself that maybe he actually believed what he was saying—that Eric hadn't needed me in the way I'd thought he had.

"Quinn?" Ava said, and I realized I'd been quiet too long, lost in my own mind. For a second, I considered asking her to clarify, but it wouldn't matter. It wouldn't change what she was saying, and it wouldn't change what I was feeling, either.

"You're right," I said finally. My throat was tight, but somehow I managed to make the words come out sounding normal.

"Nick and Eric are two different people," she said gently.

I nodded. "I know." That, I definitely did know. But me, I was the same person. Maybe that was the real problem.

Ava looked like she wanted to keep pressing, but I snagged another bite of her muffin and asked her about Cara. She was happy enough to go along with that, and I was glad, because it distracted me too. She told me all about her, even though I'd heard it before, and outlined their plans for the week. I was happy for her. I liked hearing about the good things going on in her life.

The rest of the band, and Rest in Peach, came up for lunch a little while later, and Ava and I joined them. Not long after, Nicky came back too. We smiled at each other across the room, and I was probably blushing with the way he stared at me. But he got involved in talking with his band, about what they were going to record that afternoon. I was okay with the space. It gave me some time to keep thinking about everything.

I spent the remainder of the day on the couch in the recording room. I had a book, and I flopped over and read and listened to music, letting my mind sort through things by itself. It was hard to concentrate on anything, so I didn't make myself. I just wanted to be for a while.

Nick found me later that evening. We'd all gone out to eat, and we were walking home in little groups. I hadn't had a chance to talk to Nicky—at dinner, I'd gotten shuffled around to the other side of the table from him. I'd let it happen, even though both Ty and Ava had given me raised eyebrows. I hadn't wanted to make a big deal out of it, draw any more attention to what Nick and I were doing. Not because I was embarrassed, or because I didn't want anyone to know, but because it still felt so new. I wanted to keep it as something that was only ours, for a little while longer.

Now, though, he caught up with me and slipped his hand into mine. I squeezed his fingers.

"Hey."

"Hey." He looked over at me. I could just make out the shadowy black-and-white lines of his face in the dark. "I didn't really see you at all today."

"Yeah." Now that we were walking together, and he was close enough that he could lean over and talk just for me to hear, I was wondering why I'd let any space come between us at all. It had seemed like a good idea that afternoon to stay with Escaping Indigo and . . . let things cool down? Let us have room to breathe, maybe. But having been away from him, when whatever was going on between us was still in that first-blush stage, only made me want him closer.

"Tuck told me Lissa's staying another night. Do you . . ." He took a breath and pressed his palm more firmly against mine. "Do you want to come stay at my place tonight?"

I stopped and turned to him. We were the last ones in the long, strung-out line of us, so there wasn't anyone who had to walk around us, or anyone to notice that we'd paused.

He pulled his lip between his teeth and sucked on it, before letting it go so he could speak. "It's fine if not." He smiled, but it seemed to come more from nerves than happiness. "Whatever you want."

"I'd like to." I was surprised at how quickly I'd answered, but everything seemed clearer when Nick and I were touching. Simpler. I wanted him. He wanted me. That seemed so easy.

It was as good as last time—better, maybe. We switched this time—I was still flat on my back on the bed, but it was Nicky who slipped fingers into my body, and it was . . . It had been a long time for me, and I had forgotten what this was like.

I didn't buy into that crap about penetrative sex meaning more than any other sex act, generally. But it did make me feel open and vulnerable and *seen*. Focused on.

I was breathing too hard, too fast, getting caught up in all of it, and Nick stopped, leaning over me so he could stare into my eyes. "Quinn."

I shook my head and tightened my hand around his hip. "It's good, I'm fine."

He laughed and stilled his hand. "Quinn. That is the least-convincing thing I've ever heard."

I barked out a laugh too, and the movement of it caused his fingers to rub inside me. Which turned my laugh into a moan and made me push my hips up against his palm.

His face went serious. "I don't care how we do this. Or if it doesn't work out tonight at all. It's fine with me. We can cuddle and nothing more, I don't care."

That made me relax more than anything. "It's just a lot. It feels . . ." I took a deep breath. I wasn't going to be able to explain it to him. "I can't shut my brain off. I want it, though, Nicky. I do. Like this."

He smiled gently, and then ducked his head to brush kisses along my collarbone. His fingers started moving again, the slow glide of them, and this time I shuddered and let myself dissolve into the sensations.

"What's your brain telling you?" he asked, the words muffled against my skin. The hand he didn't have between my legs moved up my side, along my ribs, soothing.

I slipped my own hands up his back, along the curve of his spine. I thought about answering his question. But with the way he was melting me into a puddle, I was sure that if I said anything, I'd say the truth. Exactly what I felt. And there was still enough rational thought left for me to think that would be a bad idea.

His lips curved against my shoulder, and his fingers pulled free of my body. "Quinn. Tell me?"

I arched up against him, helpless and needy. His hand drifted to my cock, stroking far too lightly.

"That isn't fair," I whined.

His lips drifted lower, pressing here and there across my chest, leaving warm, damp spots when his tongue flicked out. "Tell me, then." He glanced up at me. "I won't make fun. I promise." His tone was serious.

I went still all over, and he did too, freezing above me. The teasing in him was gone, and I looked up into his face. "It's telling me this is too big." I waited for him to laugh at the obvious joke, but he didn't. He kept watching me. I took a deep breath. "It feels like so much. Not just a fling. Not just for now. Like it has weight."

He went, impossibly, more still, his body poised above mine, and I was sure in that second that I had ruined this. That he would pull away, or worse, that he'd continue, but it wouldn't be the same.

Instead, he bent forward and kissed me so softly, so gently. It went on for a long time, the velvet brush of his lips on mine. He lifted a hand and held it against my face, his fingers tangling in my hair, and in the moment when we separated, I saw him staring down into my eyes.

"Want you," I whispered, even though I had half forgotten in those kisses that we had ever been on our way to something else.

He nodded and reached for the condom he'd set on the nightstand. He rolled it on, then scooted forward so his hips were nestled up against mine. Then he was slipping inside me, slowly, in a long, tight glide.

He didn't look away from me while we moved together. He fell forward onto his elbows and kept his palm to my cheek, his other hand cupping the back of my neck, while he thrust into me.

It wasn't less intense, like I'd feared it would be after I'd blurted those things out. We hadn't disconnected. The opposite, really. It was like he was breaking me apart, a piece at a time, opening up all my secret places. Exposing me.

He came first this time, pressing hard against me, snapping his hips forward, and I followed. It seemed to come from deep down, welling up instead of flashing through me, slow and harsh and forceful. It took a long time for the aftershocks to stop, for me to come back down to myself.

Afterward, we lay on top of the covers, so tangled up I couldn't tell who was holding who. I had my arms around Nicky's middle, and he had his around my neck, so my forehead pressed to his chest.

"Quinn."

"Mm-hmm?" I'd been quiet for a while. Lost in the sensation of him around me, and the way my body felt, and my own mind.

"Was that . . . okay?"

I let out a breath of a laugh. "Yeah, Nicky. It was definitely okay." I leaned forward and kissed the center of his chest.

He snuggled in a little bit closer. "Oh, good. It's just . . . you're so quiet. That's fine," he added quickly. "But I . . . I wanted to make sure it was okay. That this was okay."

"It is." I sighed. "Nicky. I meant those things. Those things I said while we were . . ."

He tensed, and then I felt him trying to *not* tense. "Yeah?"

"I . . ." I was glad I wasn't looking at his face. It was much easier to get words out this way. "I don't want only right now, Nick. I never did, I don't think. I want more than that."

He shifted slightly under me. "Like what?"

I shrugged uncomfortably. "What do you want?"

He took a deep breath, and let it out slowly, so I could feel the movement of it underneath me. I could hear his heart thumping away too, and the rhythm of it had gotten slightly faster.

"I like this," he said. "What we're doing now. Dinner and sex and hanging out and being together."

I turned that over in my mind for a second, and then I sat up, propping myself on an elbow so I could gaze down at him. "Because it's fun?"

He narrowed his eyes. "Yeah, it's fun." His voice wasn't quite steady, though.

"What about . . . beyond fun? Past fun?"

He swallowed but didn't answer, and I realized he was probably as nervous and unsure about this conversation as I was.

"I mean." I had to stop and think. It felt like my lungs were too tight, like I couldn't speak over the pounding of my heart. I hadn't known this would hit me so hard, hadn't realized it would . . . mean so much. When had I gotten in this deep? But as soon as I thought it, I figured I had probably always been in this deep. I had always liked Nick a little too much.

"I mean, do you want more than just fun? I mean, is this, what we're doing, a fling? A thing that's happening while we're both here and you're recording?"

He shook his head, his hair drifting across the pillow. "I don't know, Quinn. I always wanted more than one night with you. More than a fling." He chewed on his bottom lip, and I wanted to reach out and soothe the red spot with my thumb, but I didn't. "But that was last time. Before. I don't want . . . I don't want to get too attached and have you tell me no. And I don't know how this will work. We live apart. We have different lives."

"I'm not saying no." I was saying the exact opposite, I was pretty sure. I sat up all the way, turning to face him. The sheets were bunched around my waist, but they weren't really covering anything, and I felt exposed and vulnerable all over again.

He lifted one shoulder in a shrug. "But you might. You did last time."

I blinked. "But that was because of . . ." I raised my hand but then let it drop. I did *not* want to talk about my brother now.

He sat up too, sliding to rest against the headboard. He looked anything but comfortable, though. "I know, but . . . I'm . . . being honest. Or realistic."

"That's not being realistic," I said, before I could think. "That's being afraid."

He laughed, but it wasn't a sound of amusement at all. "And what are you doing, then? I could have been there for you—as a friend, if nothing else. All of Escaping Indigo could have been there for you. But from what I hear, you pushed everyone away. Tuck told me they didn't know Eric had died until Micah told them." He waited, giving me a chance to respond, maybe to deny it, but I didn't say anything. I couldn't. "What am I supposed to think when I hear something like that? I can't imagine it means you'll be open with me, Quinn." He lowered his voice, gentled his tone. "I'm not asking for everything at once. I know we still didn't know each other very well. But I don't want to hope for anything more than these couple of weeks, because I can't imagine you're willing to give more than that."

I drew in a shaky breath. "It's not the same. Escaping Indigo . . . Micah . . . I'm the one who takes care of them. That's my job. Not the other way around." Although I'd lost that too, really. If nothing else, this trip to the recording studio, with everyone happily paired off, had proven that. And I didn't resent it, I told myself for the millionth time. I didn't. It was just that it made me feel so alone.

"That's bullshit." Nick pinched his lips together, hard, as if he was trying to stop himself from saying anything more. It didn't work. "Getting them where they need to be as a band is your job. Making sure they have what they need. Hotel reservations and dressing rooms and lights for their shows. A place to eat. *That's* your job. Being there for them? Taking care of them? You do that because you're their friend. And friendship goes both ways." He flung his hand up. "This, what we're doing? It goes both ways. Neither of those things work if it's a one-way street. They can't. So it's not any different at all."

"It *is*." I shook my head, hard. To clear it or deny what he was saying, I wasn't sure. "And I already failed at taking care of people once. With Eric. I'm not going to do it again." Although, maybe it was too late for that. I wasn't happy about the pity party going on in my mind, but I couldn't stop it, either.

"Eric is *completely* different from all of that. But it's the same too—being a brother goes both ways. Reaching out for help goes both ways. It's not something one person can carry alone. Relationships don't work that way."

He was trying to be gentle, and reasonable. I could hear it in his voice. But I didn't *want* to hear it. "I'm worried I'll screw up again. With you. With Josh, maybe. I don't know if I can be that guy."

Nicky's eyebrows rose. "Josh is not Eric. The relationship you had with Eric—that will never be the same relationship you have with anyone else."

"I know, but—"

He swept his hand to the side in a chopping motion, cutting off my words. "And he isn't your responsibility. I'm not asking that of you. Yeah, maybe someday, if that's how this goes, and things work like that, but . . . I'm not asking you that, Quinn."

"But you kind of *are*. I'm here. I met Josh, I spent the day with him, and I . . ." I didn't actually know what I was arguing for. I didn't know what I wanted, or didn't want, I didn't know what I wanted to say. I just knew that something was *off*, strained, that something was out of place and I wanted to do something about it before it got worse. But I didn't know how to put it into words or tell Nick what I meant.

"So what you're asking me," he said very slowly, as if he wanted to be absolutely clear, "is to trust you, to allow you to get close, to let this continue, but you won't open up with me. You want me to trust that you won't hurt me again, you want to keep doing this . . . whatever we're doing, after this week. But you're basically saying, at the same time, that you don't know if you can handle it. You don't know if you can care about me. Or my son."

"What? No. That's . . ." I reached out to touch his hand, but he slid his across the bedspread so I couldn't. It was a child's gesture, petulant and stubborn, but it didn't really come across that way. It seemed . . . hurt. Like he was too tender.

"You wouldn't let me care for you before. And I get it, I really do. It was too new and too soon. But if we start this back up . . . I can't do that again. I can't have you push me away whenever anything gets rough." He lowered his voice. "I can't put that on Josh, either. And honestly, I don't think my heart can take it."

I swallowed, trying to sort this out in my mind. This wasn't how I'd imagined the evening going. I'd thought . . . When I started talking, I'd thought maybe we'd work things out, that we'd agree to . . . something, and everything would be simpler and more comfortable afterward. It hadn't occurred to me that maybe Nick wasn't thinking along the same lines as I was.

"I'm not saying any of that." But was I? I couldn't tell. I didn't know. I was so scared. "I'm not saying we shouldn't do this. I *want* to do this. I just . . ."

He smiled at me. The expression was bitter and sad, and I didn't like seeing it at all. "You're saying you'll call. You're saying we'll meet back up again soon. Like last time. Right? Last time, when what we had was really good, and we went our separate ways, and when I got home again, I waited and waited for you. Last time, when I finally gave in and called you, even though I was afraid I was pushing too hard. And you never returned my call, not even to tell me you were done. You left me hanging, wondering what I'd done wrong. Going over and over it in my mind." He squeezed his hands down on his knees. "I know I'm not supposed to let that stuff bother me. I'm an adult, I can move on. But I couldn't, Quinn. Because I liked you a lot. And I didn't know how I'd messed up."

"You didn't mess up at all." My voice was a whisper.

He nodded. "I know. But I told you, remember? I'd be an idiot to let you hurt me like that twice." He blinked. "If you want to leave, leave. If you want to stay, stay. But don't do this in-between thing. I can't take it from you. And I know you'd do it indefinitely if you could."

"I wouldn't. I . . . I don't want to leave." I wanted to reach for him again, touch him, but this time, I couldn't make myself reach for him.

"But you don't want to stay, either. You want everyone to exist outside the bubble you keep around yourself. You want to keep yourself safe in case . . . of what? In case you make a mistake? Or we do? You can't keep people at arm's length and expect them to go on loving you without conditions. It doesn't work that way."

I definitely didn't know how to answer that. And my brain had gotten tangled up on the word *love*. I opened my mouth, but then I had to close it again. I didn't have words for what I was feeling.

"You don't know what you want," I said at last. "You kiss me, you go out with me. You introduce me to your kid. Then you tell me that this is all only fun? That it can't keep going? Because ... why? Because I can't promise you everything right away?"

His expression went hard. "You could try harder. You could stop being a coward and make more of an effort."

I huffed. "Speak for yourself."

For a minute, he was perfectly still. Then he said, "I think you should go."

"Nicky ..."

"Don't." He shook his head. "Just go. Let's make it clean this time, okay?" He took an unsteady breath. "We tried it again. It didn't work. If we stop here, it'll be better. Easier. Please." For a second, I thought he would try to smile, try to make this better, but he didn't. He shook his head again. "Please go, Quinn."

I stared at him, but he'd closed himself off to me. Wrapped his arms around his middle, ducked his head to the side so he was staring at the pillows, at the place where our heads had been resting together a few minutes before. What the fuck had I done to get this so wrong? I didn't know where it had happened, and I didn't know how to fix it. I couldn't think. So I did as he said, and left. I got out of bed and grabbed my clothes, threw them on, tugging my shirt quickly over my head, stuffing my feet into my shoes while I tried to simultaneously zip up my jeans. I stumbled around, flustered and confused and embarrassed, but he didn't say anything else. I didn't even think he was watching me.

And then I was gone.

It took me until I was half a block from his house, the night cool and silent and still around me, to remember he'd driven us here, and it was a long walk back to the studio. I considered calling someone. Tuck would probably come pick me up, but he was also probably warm in bed with Lissa. Micah would come. I didn't doubt that for a second, and I wouldn't have minded getting him out of bed as much. But I didn't want to have to tell him why I was walking home instead of getting Nick to drive me. The bands had another week together at the studio, and if everyone knew Nick and I had had a falling out, it would only make everything strained and awkward. Besides, I didn't know how to explain it to myself. And maybe Micah wouldn't ask—probably, he wouldn't. He was tactful—but I didn't want to have to see him wondering.

I considered calling a taxi or something, but then I decided I'd rather have the time to think, after all. I wasn't positive of exactly where I was, so I brought up the GPS on my phone and put in the name of the studio. Ta-da. Technology at its finest. Helping you get home when you've been kicked out of your maybe-boyfriend's bed in the wee hours. I turned the sound down, so the precise voice telling me which streets to turn on was just loud enough to hear. Then I walked home.

# chapter ten

X

I t *was* a long walk, and by the time I got there, I was more confused than when I'd started out, and exhausted on top of it. The whole time, I'd tried to piece together what I should have said, what I should have done, but everything had gone so upside-down, so quickly, I couldn't sort it out. Half the time, I'd wanted to go right back, march into Nicky's house, and demand we actually talk about this, because it wasn't me who'd left this time, it was him. But I hadn't been brave enough to turn around. I'd just kept walking.

I let myself in the front entrance of the studio's house. The couch, where I'd been contemplating sleeping the day before, was right there, and it would only take me a couple of steps to collapse face-first onto it. But I wanted somewhere more private.

I crept down to the studio, leaving the lights off, feeling my way down the stairs in the dark. Once I got to the main level, it was too dark to see where I was going, so I had to switch on the hall light. But that made it easy to find my way back to the room with the stereo system and the records and CDs. There was another light switch at the end of the hall, and I flipped it off, plunging the whole studio back into darkness.

I turned on the lamp in the little room. Its glow was much softer than the hall light, and it didn't reach nearly as far. Then I lay down on the wide couch at the other side. I thought about switching the light off again, closing my eyes, and trying to sleep, but whether it was the argument with Nick or the night air, I was wide-awake.

Everything Nicky had said came back to me. Everything I'd said did too, but all of it was tangled in a jumble of words and expressions, none of it linear in my mind. This was what I'd wanted, right?

When I'd first seen Nick in the studio, I hadn't wanted to get involved with him again, because everything—*everything*—was too fragile. And then, when we *had* gotten together, I hadn't wanted to think about the future of it, because it was too big and too much, and I wasn't in a place where I could take care of anyone. I'd proven that, and I'd told him. Everything had been . . . well, it hadn't actually been too fast. We were more picking up where we'd left off a year ago. But everything was different now, and I didn't know if we were still the same together. *I* wasn't the same person I'd been then. So this should be . . . what I was aiming for. But it didn't feel right at all. It wasn't what I wanted in any way, and I was only now realizing that.

This, lying on a couch in an empty studio, by myself, was definitely not where I wanted to be. I wanted to be back in Nicky's bed. I wanted to wrap myself around him and feel him hold me. I wanted to wake up with him in the morning, and have breakfast together, and spend every minute we had together, because he was right—we didn't have too long before this bubble we were in burst, and we both went our separate ways from the studio. I should have kept my mouth shut and let it happen. But then, wouldn't we have only been repeating the past he was so afraid of?

There was a shuffle of footsteps outside the room's door, and I pulled myself away from my thoughts and looked up, expecting to see Ava in a strange déjà vu of the last time she'd come to find me here. But it wasn't her. It was Ty.

"Hi." They raised a hand in a shy half wave. "Sorry. I didn't mean to intrude. I was wandering around, and I saw the light on."

I shook my head. "It's fine." I pushed myself up on the couch so I was sitting against the arm, and gestured at the vacant other half. "Couldn't sleep?"

They shook their head. "I'm a pretty big insomniac. But I like the studio at night. It's so quiet. So different than during the day." They glanced around, taking in the records and the stereo, and the few pictures on the walls. "Like you can hear old music, a little. Like all the history comes awake and moves around."

I liked the way they put that. It *was* like that. Like the studio was more than a building or a tool for musicians to use. Like it held the music and the stories in, protected them. As if the place itself straddled the past and the present.

"Yeah. It is like that." I scrunched my toes up to make more room for them, and they sat, leaning back, hands crossed in their lap.

"What are you doing down here?"

"Tuck's with his girlfriend. I figured the couch was better."

They gave me a soft smile. "Yes. But I meant, weren't you with my drummer earlier? Or did I imagine the two of you getting into his car, making moony eyes at each other?"

I laughed. Their teasing was so gentle, and it made me comfortable, in an odd way. Like they knew exactly what they were asking, what they were pushing for, but they were going to do it in a way that made me feel safe.

"He kicked me out." I hadn't meant to say it—I'd already decided, when I chose not to call Micah, that I wasn't going to tell anyone. But I couldn't seem to help it with Ty, here in the near-dark, in the quiet.

And then I wasn't laughing anymore, and I didn't feel comfortable or safe. I was just sad and lost.

"Which of you messed up?"

I cocked my head to the side, eyeing them. "Aren't you going to take Nick's side? He's your friend."

They nodded, agreeing. Their hair, usually styled and puffed up on top of their head, was soft and loose, falling into their face. They brushed it back with a flick of their wrist. "And I love him dearly. But I know him too. I know he's impulsive and energetic, and sometimes that can be . . . a lot."

I sighed. "I'm pretty sure it was me, though. I . . ." I stopped, wondering why I was telling Ty this. Any of this. We'd known each other when we'd toured together that time, and I'd spent a lot of time with them over the last couple of weeks while we were here at the studio. I thought we might be friends, but it was the new kind of friends, the kind where we still didn't really know each other. But Ty made me, undeniably, comfortable. They actually wanted to listen to whatever I had to say. "I was scared. And I did a bad job of telling him."

"Scared of what?"

I shrugged and stared down at my lap. "Do you know what happened to my brother?"

They shifted on the couch. I still didn't want to look up. I hated that flash of pity and sadness people got on their faces when I mentioned Eric. And if Ty didn't know, I wanted to be able to explain without watching them.

They crossed their legs, folding them up and under them. They were wearing a T-shirt and pajama pants. Sleep wear. But it didn't seem to me that they'd been to bed at all.

"I know. Nicky told me. I promised not to tell anyone. He knows it's your business. But he wanted advice."

I did look up at that. "Advice on what?"

They shrugged. They were so graceful, so delicate but strong at the same time. "On what to say. Or not say. On how to comfort you if you asked. Or wanted that. I'm not the only one who knows that Nicky throws himself into everything a little bit too hard. He knows it too. And he wanted you to feel okay with him."

I groaned and let my head fall back against the couch. "Don't tell me that." I stared up at the ceiling. I blinked, and the pale orange gray of the light on the ceiling shifted and blurred, and I realized I was close to crying. I couldn't remember the last time I'd cried. Just . . . couldn't remember. It hadn't been in me. Not when Eric died. Not at his funeral. Not when I found my mom crying about him, and trying to hide it from me. It was like that part of me, the part that expressed those emotions, had been walled off, sealed away, and it was better like that. But this short time with Nicky, and it was as if he'd torn all those walls down, ripped away everything I used to protect myself, and he hadn't even been trying. He was simply good at . . . getting to me. Getting inside all the cracks and finding the deepest parts of me. Half of me loved him for it. And the other half was terrified.

"I'm not saying he's perfect, or that he doesn't make mistakes," Ty said softly. "I'm saying . . . he really wanted to try." I tipped my head forward. They were smiling, wryly. "You must have really fucked up to make him throw you out."

I opened my mouth to reply—to explain or apologize, I wasn't sure—but they held up a hand to stop me. "Why did you ask if I knew about your brother?"

I sighed. "Because I didn't take care of him. And because . . . I've been noticing, I'm not taking care of the band in the same way I used to.

I don't know . . ." I took a deep breath. Why was this so hard? It was facts. Only facts. "I don't know if I'm any good for it anymore. So I don't know if I can take care of Nicky in that way, either. Or . . . or Josh. I already failed at it once. And I don't . . . I don't know if I can do it again. I'm afraid." I raised my hands, then let them flop back into my lap. "I'm afraid. I don't want to mess up again. I don't . . . I'm not good at that."

I wasn't looking, but when Ty reached out and touched my leg, squeezing their hand around my calf, and I glanced up. They were watching me, intent, leaning forward. "Quinn. I am so sorry."

I shook my head slowly, rocking it back and forth. "I should have been there for Eric. And I wasn't. I should be there for the band, but I'm not. Nick made sure to point that out tonight." I gave Ty a wobbly smile. "I don't . . . I don't want to promise Nicky and Josh that I'll be there when they need me. Because there's a good chance I won't. I don't know what I can do. I don't know if I can do this again."

Ty sighed, but they didn't sit back or pull away. "Your brother was an adult, right? A grown man?"

I nodded.

"Do you honestly think you could have stopped him from doing what he wanted to do? Do you honestly think that if you'd been there, you would have changed his mind? Made him want something else?"

The question froze me, and it took me a minute to answer. "I don't know."

"Do you blame Micah for what happened to your brother?"

I shook my head hard. "Of course not."

"Then why are you blaming yourself? If Micah, who, I think I'm right in saying, was your brother's best friend? If he couldn't change it, why do you think you could have?"

A shiver ran through me, and I tried to shake it away. "I don't know." My voice was rough and soft, a whisper. "I just think I should have been there. I should have done more."

Ty sighed and sat back, but not far. Their hand still lay between us on the couch. "Listen to me, Quinn. Nicky doesn't want you to take care of him. Not . . . unevenly like that. He's looking for a partner, not a babysitter. Not for him, and not for Josh."

"Yeah, but—"

They held up their hand. "There are a lot of ways to fuck up a kid." They let out a dry laugh. "Lot of ways. I didn't know your brother. But when I talk to Micah, when he isn't talking about Bellamy, he's talking about Eric. He loved him. And I didn't know your brother, but damn do I like Micah. He's the best sort of person. From everything he's said, your brother was that type of person too, and I'm inclined to believe him. I imagine he was like that because of how *you* taught him to be. I don't think you fucked him up. I think you brought him up well. I don't think it would have mattered whether you were around more or not. You showed him he could be anything, do anything, that he wanted. If you'd stayed, he'd never have thought to aim for that. And I still don't think you would have been able to persuade him away from a thing that made him feel good."

My throat was tight, and I couldn't do anything but shake my head.

"You think you're going to fuck up," Ty said gently, "but you've proven over and over again that you can care for people, with the way you care for your band."

I kept shaking my head. "They've all got someone else to do that for them now."

Ty sighed, and it sounded sad. "Oh, Quinn."

I gave a watery laugh. "I know how bad that sounds. I just... They don't need me anymore. What happens when Nicky doesn't need me? Or what happens when I show him I can't care for anyone, that I don't know how to do this anymore?" I wrapped my hand in my T-shirt and tugged, wishing for something to break, or something to hold on to. "That was always what I was best at. Taking care of people. It was what I *did*, it was my whole life. And in one shot I proved I'd never been as good at it as I'd thought. That it was a lie."

"Quinn, Quinn. That isn't true at all. If you talked to your friends, you'd know that. They still need you. They've just found other people to need too. It isn't the same thing, though. What you do for them, the friend you are to them—no one is ever going to take that place."

Their words hit me like a series of soft blows. Inconsequential at first, something I could brush off and away. But the more they talked, the harder the words fell, and they bruised me, breaking past those ridiculous shields I had up. Breaking past all my logic and reason, and right into the place where I kept my sadness, my hurt and my grief. I still didn't believe it, not really. But I hadn't realized how badly I'd wanted to hear that, either. To have that reassurance.

When Ty finished talking, I stared at them for a second. Then I tipped my head forward, let my shoulders slump, and I cried.

They were good about it. They put their hand on my shoulder and rubbed soothing circles, but they didn't try to calm me any more than that, and they didn't say anything else. They let me spill out all that compacted, hidden-away sadness.

"I'm scared," I mumbled finally. Or I meant to mumble it, but I was crying harder than I'd thought I could, and the words came out in loud, choked gasps. "I don't know what I'm doing." I wondered, vaguely, if they knew how difficult it was for me to admit that. I was supposed to be the strong one, the support. Not the person who was scared. But saying I was afraid was all I'd been doing lately.

Ty laughed gently and squeezed my shoulder. "None of us do, really. But I know Nicky thinks the world of you. I know when he met you, whenever he talked about you, it was like you were the best thing since sliced bread. Like you lit him up from the inside. And when you didn't come back to him, when he didn't hear from you, he tried to hide it, but he was crushed. He isn't unreasonable or clingy. That's not Nicky. But . . . he knew he'd found a good thing with you. He knew he wanted to be with you. And then it got taken away. And he was hurt."

I looked up at them. I expected them, still, to be angry, to try to defend Nicky. To tell me I was wrong. But they weren't. They were being so kind.

"I don't like seeing him hurt," Ty continued. "I get being scared, though. And I'm not saying taking on a relationship isn't scary. It's fucking terrifying." It startled a laugh out of me, and Ty smiled. "And taking on someone's kid is . . . I can't imagine, actually. It's huge. And you might make mistakes. Nick will for sure make mistakes.

But I think you did a really *good* job with your brother. And if you wanted to, if what you and Nick have grew to that, you could do a really good job with Josh."

I wiped my palm across my face. "I think it's probably too late for that. After Nicky kicking me out and all."

Ty sank back against the couch. "I don't know. I think being scared runs both ways. And I bet Nicky's just scared that you're going to disappear again. You can't blame him. You already did it once, and he wants to trust you—I think he does trust you—but the fear of being hurt, of being left, is pretty big. It's hard to get over. And he doesn't have any reason to believe you won't do it again, because it's easier. Because it's safer."

"I didn't want to leave him. I . . ." I sighed. God, I was tired. I hadn't realized I could be more exhausted than before, but having emotions was draining. "I proved that too, didn't I? That I'd leave again, tonight. I mean, he was the one who made me go, but the whole conversation, everything I said . . . I panicked. And I didn't know how to tell him."

"Did you actually want to tell him? Or did you want to run?"

I shot them a sharp glare. "You're disturbingly perceptive. Anyone ever tell you that?"

They smiled. "A few people. Gets me in trouble."

"So what do I do?"

"What do you want to do?"

I closed my eyes. "I don't know. Not this. I don't want it . . . to be like this."

They pushed themselves up and stood over me. "Then talk to him. Just . . . talk. It's not a promise of anything. It's only a conversation."

I sank down further on the couch. "What if he doesn't want to talk?"

They shrugged. "That's his right. But I think he will. Maybe let him have a few days, first." They walked over to the lamp and flicked it off. I didn't know how they could see in the dark, but they didn't seem to have a problem. "Now get some rest. Talking won't do any good if you turn your brain to mush from lack of sleep."

They left without another word—and without bumping into anything. I didn't think, until after they'd gone, to wonder why they were here, at the studio, instead of in their own house. I pushed it from my mind for the moment and closed my eyes and, although I thought it might still be impossible, drifted off to sleep.

# chapter eleven

X

When Nick arrived the next morning for recording, he avoided me. We all had lunch together that afternoon, like we'd been doing most days, and Nick sat at the other end of the room and seemed like he was trying not to look at me. Bellamy kept shooting me glances, looking back and forth between the two of us with his eyebrows raised. I just shook my head. I'd tell him everything later, maybe. When it made more sense to me.

Nicky could have seemed petulant, childlike, and I could have felt worn down by how upset he was. But I kept thinking about what Ty had told me the night before. How I probably wasn't the only one who was scared. How I wasn't the only one protecting myself from being hurt. And instead of feeling guilty, or angry, I was sad I'd been the cause of that. That somehow, Nicky and I, two people who seemed to genuinely like each other, had managed to hurt each other so much.

I wanted to talk to him. And I didn't. I didn't know where to start, or what to say. Rest in Peach wasn't going to be in the studio much longer, so this was my chance to be in the same place as Nick, and I needed to take it. But I wasn't sure how. I didn't know what to say that would reassure either one of us. And frankly, I still wasn't convinced that I was capable of caring for someone, of starting a relationship, despite what Ty and I had talked about.

Ava solved it for me, like she'd been solving my problems all week. After lunch, everyone drifted away in little groups, and I stood up to . . . do something. I still wasn't sure what. Ava caught me in the hallway and pulled me aside.

I looked back to the kitchen, where Cara, who had flown in yesterday, was still sitting at the table. I'd said hello to her, but I'd been too wrapped up in my own thoughts to be much company.

"Don't you want to be with Cara?" I asked, hoping to escape or something.

Ava ignored me. "What's going on with you and Nick?"

I shrugged and rubbed the back of my neck. "We had a fight, I guess."

"You guess? Over what?" She narrowed her eyes at me. "Over what we talked about, you and me?"

"Sort of?"

"Jesus, Quinn." She sighed and ran her hand through her hair, making her bangs stand up. "I didn't think you were going to take what I said and use it to break up with him."

"I didn't! I . . . You were right, about it being a big responsibility. Not only Josh, but Nicky. And thinking carefully about whether I wanted to do that and everything."

"I was thinking about *myself*." She shook her head. "I wasn't . . . Yeah, it is a big responsibility, and yeah, it is a big decision, even at the beginning of a relationship, but god, you're made for that. You take care of all of us, and you're good at it. And I think it makes you happy. I hope it does. Because you make all of us feel safe, all the time. You're our rock."

My mouth opened and closed, but no sound came out. I liked it when Ava was blunt, because I couldn't misconstrue what she was saying. But it meant when she said something like that, something that good, I had to believe it.

"Nick and Josh would be *lucky* to have you in their lives. Whether or not it works out between you and Nick in the end. And I know you, despite how fucking hard you work to keep yourself all bundled up inside. You'd be lucky to have them too, both of them, and you'd love it." She lowered her voice. "You'll love him and his kid. I can see it in your eyes when you talk about it, so don't bother telling me I'm wrong. Maybe it's not love yet, but I think it could be, if you give it time."

I closed my eyes so she couldn't read anything else there, but I answered her with the truth anyway. "You're not wrong."

She shook her head at me, as if I was absolutely exasperating. "Then why aren't you trying to apologize to him right now? Or talk to him?"

I wanted to joke and ask her what made her think I was the one who needed to apologize, but I couldn't do it.

I didn't answer her question, either. "I didn't think ... you needed me anymore. You or Bellamy or Tuck or Micah."

Her brow scrunched up into a confused frown. "You mean, like, as our manager? Because we're definitely not firing you."

I shook my head. "No. I mean, I didn't think ... I thought you had other people to take care of you now." I couldn't stop repeating, over and over in my mind, what she'd said. *"You're our rock."*

"Quinn." Her voice sounded like it was about to fracture. She glanced into the kitchen, then grabbed my arm and tugged me farther down the hall, so we were completely out of sight. "Why would you think that?" she asked, her tone lower. She was standing closer to me too, so I could feel her breath on my chin when she stared up at me.

"Because." I ran my hand over my eyes, pinching the bridge of my nose, giving myself time to think. "It's just that I've been seeing all of you, all together here, and I've been thinking about Eric, and how much I fucked that up. And I'm okay, I really am. But Micah's moving on, and Bellamy doesn't need me to calm him down anymore, because he's got Micah, and you went and found Cara, and Tuck and Lissa are so attached there's no space between them ..." I trailed off, because Ava had a horrified expression on her face, her mouth hanging open. "I'm happy for you," I added quickly. "I'm so happy, and I'm not jealous, I'm not. I'm just ..."

Her face softened. "Feeling left out?"

I sighed and nodded. "Yeah."

She ran her hand up and down my arm, soothing me. "We're all being idiots because we're new in love and stuff." She made a face at her own phrasing, but then she shrugged. "Well, except Tuck and Lissa. They're gooey all the time. But I know you know how that is."

"I do. That's why I said I'm not jealous. I'm not."

"It doesn't mean you can't feel left out, though. I'm sorry we did that to you."

I raised my hand. "No, oh my god, don't be sorry. That's not what I wanted at all."

She crossed her arms in front of her. "Well, I am."

"It's not even that I feel left out. I don't. You all always make a place for me. It's that I feel like you don't need me as much anymore. Because you don't." And I couldn't help but think that had something to do with how I'd failed Eric. If I'd failed him, had I failed the band too? Had I always been bad at this? I didn't know. But I didn't know who I was when I wasn't taking care of people, either. So I was caught between wanting to do that, and knowing it might all be false.

Ava was shaking her head at me though. "We have other people in our lives now. But that doesn't mean we don't need you, Quinn. We always need you. Not as a roadie, either. Not only, not by a long shot."

I frowned and opened my mouth, getting ready to argue or something, but she stopped me.

"Do you think Bellamy and Tuck and I weren't taking care of each other before you came along?"

"I . . ." I didn't know how to answer. It was so simple, but I hadn't actually ever thought about it.

"We were, because we're friends. I know, it's super fucking cheesy, but that's, you know, what friends do." She shrugged. A pink blush rose over her cheeks and up her neck. "We need you because you're our friend. That's never going to change."

I was all choked up again. God, this was getting embarrassing already. Ava whapped me on the arm affectionately, and for a minute we just stood there together and tried to get ourselves under control.

"For the record," she said at last, "you're super fucking good at taking care of the band. And you're really good at taking care of people. Maybe you messed up with Eric. I don't know. But you've never messed up with anyone else. And I wouldn't want anyone else but you."

It should have stung unbelievably, to hear her admit that I might actually have messed up with Eric. To have her confirm my worst fears. But it was the opposite. It was like a giant rush of relief. Maybe I *had* done things wrong. Maybe I should have tried harder. But Ava still loved me, and she still wanted me. Escaping Indigo, Micah, they still wanted me. I might have fucked up, or I might not have. But maybe it didn't make all the ways I cared about people a lie.

"Thank you," I said, sincerely, and she gave me an awkward one-armed hug.

"I'm not really cut out for these heart-to-hearts," she said dryly, and I laughed.

"You do just fine."

She looked up at me. "So what are you going to do about Nicky, then?"

Oh god, that was right. This conversation had been about Nick, before I'd made it about everything else. "I don't know."

"But you do want to be with him, right?"

I took a deep breath and nodded. "Yeah. I do. But I ... I'm scared."

She poked me on the shoulder, startling me. "Everybody's scared. No one goes into a relationship thinking it's going to be easy. It won't be. But it'll be worth it." She turned and glanced back toward the kitchen, where Cara was sitting. "Don't fuck it up. I know how easy that is to do. Don't let it get too bad. Go get him now while you still can."

X

Getting Nicky alone was easier said than done, though, and I didn't actually think he was actively avoiding me. But Rest in Peach was all jazzed about being nearly done recording, and Escaping Indigo and Ben and everybody else in the studio were riding the excitement. Nick was in the studio all day, and there wasn't a chance for me to talk to him. Then we ordered pizza for dinner—from a super posh place, because this was LA, but certainly none of us were actually too posh for pizza itself—and we crowded back into the kitchen and living room at Ben's, and everybody talked at once. It wasn't the place for a conversation like the one I imagined I was going to have to have with Nick.

I wandered out onto the back balcony instead of trying to get his attention anymore right then. I'd been planning to come out here since we'd arrived, but I never had. Now I wondered why I'd spent any time moping in my room or down in the studio, when this was obviously a much better place for melodramatic self-contemplation. It looked out over the small, vibrantly green backyard—which was really more the side of a hill than anything—and the neighborhood, down to where the houses started to turn into businesses, and the foot traffic got heavier. It would be easy to fall in love with a place like this. So self-contained and alive and in the middle of things, all at once.

I was disappointed I hadn't found a way to talk to Nick. I hadn't really asked, truth be told. I just couldn't make myself. Not in front of everyone like that. Not when he had every reason to refuse me. I figured I'd try again in a little while, when everyone was more settled and calming down. Or, if that didn't work, I'd try to find a moment when he was by himself tomorrow, or if I couldn't, maybe I'd go really dramatic and show up on his doorstep tomorrow evening after recording. Although that was probably a step too far. I'd have died if anyone did that to me. But Nicky would probably like the flair in it. The obvious display of emotion. And I would do it for him, if it was what he needed.

But I didn't have to, because a few minutes after I'd stepped out onto the balcony, the sliding door opened again, the soft whoosh of the glass sliding in its tracks making me turn around, and Nick was there. He paused and shut the door behind him, but he did it by feel, never letting me out of his sight. Then he stepped forward to where I was standing off to the side, so no one inside the house could see me.

"I can go." I wanted to slap myself. I'd gotten the privacy to talk to him, and I was offering to leave.

He shook his head. He had a beer in his hand, and he rolled it between his palms while he stared at me. Then he shook his head again, like he was deciding something. "No, I'll go."

I reached out without thinking as he turned, and caught his arm. "Don't. Please."

For a long second, he didn't turn, and I figured he'd slip out of my hold and walk back through the door. It hadn't struck me, until right this moment, when he stood between leaving and listening to me, how very much I needed him. How very much I wanted to be with him, how much I wanted to apologize, for all of it. I'd known. But I hadn't realized how much. I hadn't realized how important he'd become. Not a fling—not that I'd ever thought of him that way. Not a *right now* type of friend. Nick was someone I wanted in my life always, if I could get that. I wanted him near me as long as I could get. And I wanted to tell him I regretted every single time I'd messed up what was between us.

I held my breath until he faced me again. It was a weight inside me, as if I'd crammed all my worries and fears and wants into that single lungful of air.

It only took him a step to get to the balcony's railing, to stand beside me. He set his drink down at his feet and leaned forward, elbows resting on the wrought iron railing.

"What was it you wanted, Quinn?"

God, I couldn't even speak. Now I had him here, he was willing to listen to me, and I couldn't make words come out.

"I talked to Ty," I blurted out. "And Ava."

He stared out over the lawn. "And what did they say?" he asked, his voice easy, unconcerned. I saw the tightness in his shoulders, though, the tension he held just under his skin.

"Ty said . . ." I wasn't sure if I should admit this or not, but I'd already gotten into it. "Ty said you were probably as scared as me. And Ava . . ." I didn't know why this was still so hard. "Ava said she needed me. That I . . . that I take care of her and the band. And that I would be good at taking care of you."

He nodded, the movement quick and sharp. He didn't look at me. "Is that what you want? To take care of me?"

I shuddered out a breath and went for broke. "I want us to take care of each other."

He was quiet for so long after that, I thought about leaving again. If I slipped away, this could be over, this painful awkwardness and embarrassment and hurt ended. But I didn't want that. Nicky had told me, that night we went out to dinner, and before, that he'd wished he'd had some kind of end to what was between us. A marker, maybe. A way to see it was finished. I didn't want us to be finished. Not now, not anytime in the future. But if that was what was happening, if what we had was ending, then I wanted . . . I wanted a resolution to this too. I wanted to see it out, all the way until the end.

I didn't want to have the same regrets. So I stayed, standing next to him, and I didn't say a thing.

"I talked to Ty today too," he said at last, his voice pitched low and soft. "They told me they talked to you. They told me . . . some of what you talked about."

I swallowed hard. I wished I'd brought my own drink out, so I could have something to do with my hands. "I'm sorry, Nick. I'm so sorry."

He twisted so he faced me, finally. "Why didn't you explain that to me? About . . . feeling guilty about your brother, and worrying about not being able to take care of people? About being scared about . . . us? About being scared of letting me down?" His tone was somewhere between accusatory and . . . not quite guilty, but maybe sad.

"Why did you agree to any of this if you only wanted a couple of weeks?" I tossed back. "Why did you start this back up again if you were afraid of what would happen at the end?"

"Because I missed you," he snapped. He looked away again. "I wanted you." His voice was lower now, almost a whisper. "But I missed you too. And seeing you again, being near you, it reminded me of how much I liked being with you." He glanced up at me, then away. "You didn't want this to go on more than a few weeks, either."

I shook my head. "That's not true. I always did. I just didn't think I could."

"You thought it would be better to protect me by leaving again?"

I shrugged. "Maybe. I don't know, Nick. I wasn't thinking clearly. I'm still not." I sighed. "This isn't what I wanted to say. I don't want to be . . . I don't want to be defensive. I want to apologize. What I want to say is, I messed up. Now, and before. Last time. And I'm so sorry I hurt you."

His mouth opened, like he wanted to argue or respond somehow, but then he pressed his lips together.

For a long minute, we stood together, staring out at the miniscule yard and the back of the hill. Not far away, I could see more houses, creeping up other hillsides. Glass walls and small pools, narrow balconies like this one. The houses around here only got more and more expensive, more elaborate. I wondered how Ben had ever managed to afford a place like this to begin with, let alone turn it into this massive studio. Maybe he'd been born here. Or maybe he was simply very good at what he did, and had earned it.

"Your band—your friends—love you," Nick said at last, breaking the silence. His voice was still low, and he didn't turn toward me. "You're not superfluous, or whatever you think you are. It doesn't work that way. Like I said before."

I sighed and rested my hands on the railing, close to his, but not quite touching. "I know. Ava . . . made that pretty clear."

He did face me then. "The reason I was so angry, so afraid, the reason I asked you to leave—none of it had anything to do with your band or your brother. It was just that I didn't want to get hurt again."

I thought about what Ava had said this afternoon. "Do you think it's possible to go into something like this and absolutely know you won't get hurt?" I wasn't trying to direct him toward an answer. I honestly wanted to know what he thought about that.

He shook his head. "No. But I think it's possible to take precautions. And that probably means not getting involved with someone who's already hurt you once before."

I closed my eyes against the sunlight and his gaze. "I never wanted to hurt you."

"I know. But you did, Quinn."

I blinked and found that he'd stepped closer to me.

"I'm not asking you to promise me this will work out perfectly."

I raised my eyebrows at him and smiled. "That's almost what you were asking last night."

He drew in a sharp breath, then paused, and shook his head. "I know. I was confused and worried. But I wanted too much, too fast. All or nothing. Not a maybe. I shouldn't have asked for that. And," he added, "I shouldn't have made you walk home alone. I didn't think of it until maybe an hour later. I'm sorry, Quinn."

It was me who shook my head this time. I ignored the bit about me walking home too. "You didn't push at all last time. I *wanted* to see you again, back then. I wanted . . . I wanted whatever was between us to go somewhere. I didn't mean to let it stop. But I was . . . I panicked so bad, Nick. It was like everything I knew about myself was a lie. And I didn't want you to see it. But it didn't have anything to do with you pushing too hard."

He turned to face me. "I don't understand. Why would what your brother did be your fault?"

I shrugged. I wanted to tumble inside myself, bury down, and hide all of my flaws and all of the mistakes I'd made. But that was what had gotten me here in the first place. "Because it made me rethink everything I knew about my life. I take care of people. That's my job. It's what I do. It's what I'm . . . It's what I thought I was good at. Some people want to be musicians, and some people want to be lawyers, and I . . . I didn't plan to take care of people, but it's what I do and I like it. But I didn't take care of Eric. I wasn't there when he needed someone."

"But he did have someone," Nicky said, so gentle it splintered something inside me. "He had Micah. And he had you. He could have reached out to you. But he didn't. Because . . . I'm guessing he didn't think he needed help. Even if you'd been there, I don't know that you'd have been able to change anything. I know he must have known he could reach out to you if he needed. You were always there for him, Quinn."

It was the same thing Ava had said, and Ty, and Micah. Maybe it was finally clicking. Maybe if I heard it enough, I'd start to believe it.

I reached for him, blindly, seeking comfort, although I was pretty sure I didn't deserve it, and he stepped forward and wrapped his arms around me. I put my head down on his shoulder, and he swayed back and forth, like he might have with Josh, soothing me. His hands were warm and solid against my back, his body strong, so I knew I could lean on him and he'd hold me up.

"I don't want to let you down," I mumbled into his shirt. "I don't want . . . I want to be able to take care of you. And Josh deserves someone who won't let him down, either."

He brushed his hand through my hair. "I love that you want to protect Josh. But that's my job right now. I don't think you'd let him down anyway. But still. And as for me." He dipped his face and kissed the top of my head. "I don't want you to take care of me. Or not just one way. I want us to be partners in this, okay? We take care of each other. That's how it works."

I moved away enough to see him, to look into his eyes. "You still want this to work? Us. Even after last night. For more than . . . for after this, after we're done recording?"

He smiled, shy and uncertain but so hopeful it made me all tingly inside. "Yes. I think . . . I'm pretty sure I wanted this to work between us from the second I saw you. All in charge and ordering rock stars around and making sure we all had enough lunch, that someone set my kit up right for me, that Bellamy wasn't going out to smoke without his coat on. God, I fell for you right then. And I wanted . . . You took care of everyone else. I wanted to take care of you."

I couldn't think how to answer that, couldn't figure out how to put everything inside of me, everything I was feeling, into words. All the confusion and the happiness and the worry and sadness and the sheer, unbelievable joy. So I kissed him instead. Moved forward and pressed my lips against his, held his hips. It wasn't a deep kiss. Just . . . touch and closeness, and the desire to be near him. He tucked his hands into my back pockets and kissed me back.

When we pulled apart, he was still smiling, but this time it was wider and more sure, that grin I was used to. I reached up, brushed his hair out of his eyes, and smiled back at him. "I never wanted to end things between us. Not now. Not the first time. I just got scared."

He sobered. "I know. And the first time, I really do understand that. I didn't belong there with you, not then. But this time . . . There are two of us in this thing, you know? So you need to talk to me, instead of deciding what's best and backing away. And . . ." He ducked his head and looked up at me through his bangs. "I need to listen. Instead of flipping out."

I laughed softly. "Yeah. Well, we can work on that."

He nodded back. "I'm still scared you're going to hurt me, Quinn. But I think I'd rather try than not."

I hesitated, but I had to ask. I had to be sure. "What changed your mind?"

He smiled and shrugged. "I think we're going to try very hard not to do the same things as last time. Try not to mess up. Try to talk to each other. I think we're already better at that than we were last time." He let out a sharp breath. "I think I knew that days ago. That it was different now. But I wasn't letting myself remember that last night because . . . I was angry, and I wasn't thinking. I panicked. But I knew it days ago. I was afraid to admit it, though. Afraid to hope this might actually work this time."

I took a deep breath. "Me too."

"Come home with me tonight? I swear I don't want to move too fast. But we can . . . talk about stuff, logistics, how this might work? And . . . I really want to spend some time with you, alone, before you go back to San Diego."

"Yeah. Yes. Please." I was still scared, about all of it. I still didn't think I was going to be very good at this. And I was still afraid I was going to mess it all up. But that short period of uncertainty with Nicky, after knowing exactly how good it could be between us, had been awful. And like he'd said, I wanted to try my best to make sure it didn't happen again.

We left before anyone else. Ty gave me a knowing look and a slight smile, and Ava patted me on the back and gave me what I was pretty sure was close to a leer. Everyone knew where we were headed and what we were probably going to get up to, and it should have been embarrassing, but I didn't care. I had Nicky's hand in mine, and it felt incredible, and that was all that mattered.

X

I was exhausted from the day, and the night I'd spent on the couch, and Nick was worn out from recording and having Josh around. By some silent agreement, we didn't put any pressure on our time together, or on each other. Since neither of us had gotten to eat any of the pizza at Ben's and we were still craving it, we cooked together, like we had the first day. Nick had a frozen pizza crust, and we piled whatever ingredients we found appealing on it, and then wandered over to the couch with our drinks while we waited for it to cook.

I might have dozed for a few minutes. Nick shook me awake gently.

"Here." He handed me a plate with a couple of slices on it and sat next to me. "Eat before you fall asleep, or you'll wake up at midnight starving."

I leaned over and kissed his cheek, which made him blush. He covered it by taking a bite of his own pizza.

I brought our plates to the kitchen when we were done, and stuffed them in the dishwasher. That was good enough for now. I wanted to get back to Nicky.

"Take me to bed now?" I asked, when I was sitting beside him again.

He laughed. "You mean you don't want to fuck me over the couch?"

I stared up at him. His eyes were dark, and he was teasing, but there was something deep and intense in his gaze, something that hooked me and wouldn't let me go. "I don't care what we do," I blurted out honestly. "I don't care if you just want to lie next to me. I only want to be near you."

His smile faded, but he didn't look unhappy. With his free hand, he cupped my face, his thumb sliding over my cheek. Then he bent forward and kissed me, lightly, tenderly. My forehead, my eyelids, the bridge of my nose. My mouth.

"I could fall in love with you," he said softly when he pulled back.

My heart pounded hard against my chest. "Yeah?"

He nodded and looked down, tracing his thumb over my bottom lip.

I caught his hand, stilling it. "Me too. It'd be easy."

"Maybe we should plan to do that, then."

I laughed, and his lip quirked up at the side. "Yeah. Maybe we should."

I thought we might end up only sleeping tonight, without anything else after all, despite the way Nick had laughed. That would be fine with me. I wanted to be near Nicky. I didn't care what form that took. I didn't think he cared much, either. But I was more awake now, and when I followed him into his bedroom, I caught his hand, tugged him to me, and kissed him.

We shed our clothes and climbed into his ridiculously silky sheets, and he held me against him. It was simpler, this time, but no less fantastic. We ran our hands over each other and brought our bodies together, and finally he reached down and took us both in his palm. Then we rocked together, sharing kisses, panting into the darkness. When he came, warm against my skin, he made a sound somewhere between a moan and a sob, and I leaned forward and kissed him so I could taste it. It tasted of happiness and relief, worry and nerves, satisfaction and comfort. I kissed him and tried to give all of those things back, to let him know I felt them too. Then he squeezed his hand gently around me, and I could only push against him, needing him.

Afterward, we lay together, languid and lazy and too tired to move. This time when he kissed me, he was smiling, and it tasted even better. I could feel the curve of his mouth against mine, the sharp zing of sweetness that happiness brought.

He snuggled into my side and pressed that same smile against my shoulder. "I'm glad you're here."

I could have teased him about how sentimental that sounded, but I didn't. I didn't want to tease him. And it made me happy, like he'd poured honey into my veins, and it was seeping into every part of me—slow and steady and sweet, the most wonderful, intoxicating sensation. "Me too."

"When are you going back on tour?" he asked quietly.

I shifted so I was facing him, my arm around his shoulders. "Maybe six months? It isn't set in stone yet. But the record label will probably want them out a couple months after the album drops. You?"

"Sooner than that. We're going out with the album. Not the best idea ever, but Ty wants to get back on the road, and I don't blame them. We'll probably do a world tour this time."

I brushed his hair back and kissed his forehead. "That's a good thing. A big step."

"Yeah." He was quiet for a moment, like he was going to sleep. Then he said, his voice soft, "When will I see you?"

Ahh. I took a deep breath. "Let's do weekends first? Make sure we actually like being with each other for all that time?" I couldn't imagine not, and Nicky frowned like he couldn't either, and wanted to argue it. But he nodded instead.

"I have Josh on weekends. So maybe we can do every other weekend, and some weekdays? Then we can have time to ourselves too."

I nodded. "I like that."

We were still and quiet for a while, lying there together.

"I don't want to break this," I said finally, my words only a breath of sound between us. "I don't want it to . . . be overwhelming and to have me panic over something stupid and make the same mistakes."

"I know. I don't want that either." He brushed his hand up my neck, into my hair, tugging gently. "I don't think that's going to happen. I mean . . ." He gave a laugh. "We'll argue about stuff. I don't have any doubt about that. But I think . . . we'll be more careful this time. Don't you?"

I nodded. I did think that. Especially now. Now that I realized what an idiot I'd been. Or was starting to realize I'd been. "Maybe we can meet up while we're both on tour too? Or . . . maybe we could meet up while one of us is on tour? Stay together for a while? If things are still working between us?"

He perked up at that. "You want to?"

"If I can. If we decide it's a good idea. If it's okay with the rest of your band, and there's space for me."

He grinned and pressed a kiss to the side of my neck. "You make me happy. They know that. It'll be okay with them."

God, how had I gotten this lucky? I didn't know. And I didn't want to question it.

We talked a bit more, in half sentences and murmurs. Then we drifted off like that, wrapped around each other.

# epilogue

*r*est in Peach finished recording a few days before Escaping Indigo.
It wasn't quite an ending—we'd still be around for a while, and
most of Rest in Peach lived close enough that they could come and see
us again before we left if they wanted. But it felt like an end. Closure,
a resolution to the time we'd had together, tucked into the close,
private, cocoon-like space of the recording studio. Hidden from the
world, surrounded by music, and friends, and lovers.

I could admit that I was getting pretty sentimental over all of it,
even though, in the grand scheme of things, it had only been a couple
of weeks. It had been important, though. For all of us, for all the
reasons.

Somehow, Tuck and Ty decided the best thing to do to celebrate
was make everyone go to the beach. Nicky was excited about it. He
bounced around like a little kid at the idea, and I had to struggle not
to make any remarks about how similar he was to his son.

"We can go to the beach anytime," I said, while he stood in my
bedroom at the studio and I dug my swim trunks out of my duffel
bag. "You live down the street." I didn't live far from it myself, in San
Diego. A short drive and I was there. I saw it any time I went to Ava's
or Tuck's houses.

Nick flopped over onto my bed and grinned up at me. "But it's
nice out."

I quirked an eyebrow at him. "We're in LA. When is it not
nice out?"

He caught my wrist in his hand, his fingers circling my pulse
point. "We get to go together. With everyone. I haven't ever been to
the beach with you. I want to see what you look like in the waves.
With sand between your toes."

I blushed. "You do not." I'd found my swim trunks, and wanted to hold them up in front of myself like some flimsy shield.

"Oh." Nick's smile deepened. "I do."

I tackled him and pinned him to the bed. I couldn't help myself.

We were late to the beach, of course. It wasn't only Nick and me who had gotten distracted. Cara was still here, and she and Ava were spending an extraordinary amount of time making up for all that long-distance relationship-ing. And Danni and Ty were late meeting us at the studio, because Ty had been having some kind of fashion crisis. I couldn't fathom what it had been. When they showed up, Ty looked stunning, decked out in a sleek black bathing suit and a swishy white-and-black skirt.

Between them and all the other musicians looking *very* much like rock stars, and Ben with his colorful tattoos, I felt unstylish and ungainly and out of place.

"This is why I like San Diego," I grumbled to Nick while we laid out beach towels, and Cara hoisted up a couple of umbrellas so we wouldn't all burn under the too-bright California sun. "It's more laid-back. No one cares what you look like or what you're wearing." Okay, so that was a bit of an exaggeration. But at least San Diego was home.

Nick straightened up and stared at me. "What are you talking about? What do you look like?"

I gestured at myself, my wide shoulders, scruffy beard, the plain green T-shirt I was wearing. My flip-flops, worn and starting to fray. My battered, definitely not designer sunglasses. "Not like you. Not like . . ." I gestured at Danni, perfectly comfortable in a bikini, splashing through the waves with Tuck, who had this vibe to him, this way he carried himself, that said *famous* in big, bold letters.

Nick frowned. "Since when do you care about that?"

I sighed and sat down in the shade, my butt on the towel but my feet on the sand. It was blisteringly hot, until I buried my toes and got to the damp coolness underneath. "I don't. I just . . ." I just wanted to be as cool as everyone else. I wanted anyone who saw us to think I fit with the rest of them. It wasn't about looks so much as . . . style. Or . . . comfort. Or some intangible thing that the bands and Cara, Micah, and Ben had and I didn't, quite.

He sat next to me and kissed my cheek. "What about them?" He pointed at Elliot, who had slathered himself with so much sunscreen I could see the white streaks across his shoulders and his cheeks. Then Nick flicked his fingers at Micah and Bellamy. They were standing right where the waves reached, dancing back every time the water got close, kicking up sparkling droplets, clinging to each other. They looked ridiculous. Ridiculous and happy. Not like rock stars. Simply . . . like people enjoying each other. Bellamy tipped his head back and laughed, long and loud, as if he had no control over the sound. Micah grinned, and when Bellamy stopped laughing, Micah leaned forward and kissed him. They stayed still then, letting the waves wash around their ankles as if they didn't notice at all. They were too lost in each other.

I glanced over at Ava and Cara. They were standing by the cooler, sorting through, searching for a drink. Cara had her hand in Ava's, and she kept lifting it and kissing her palm. At first, it seemed like Ava was ignoring it, like it was so commonplace she could forget it was happening. But then she found the soda she wanted and shut the cooler, setting the drink on the closed lid. She straightened, turned to Cara, and took both of Cara's hands in hers. She brought them up and kissed each palm, lingering, letting her lips stay against the skin for a handful of seconds. Cara flushed bright red and laughed. Then she leaned her forehead against Ava's and said something too softly for me to hear. Whatever it was had Ava blushing back at her and grinning.

Lissa had gone down and joined Danni and Tuck, and Elliot was making his way over too, despite his paranoia about the sun. Lissa had a Frisbee, and she held it up as a question. Tuck bounced over and kissed her cheek, then stole the Frisbee from her and ran off down the beach, laughing like mad. Lissa raced after him, until he turned and hurled the Frisbee backward. Lissa caught it and tossed it to Danni, who sent it sailing toward Elliot.

Not too far from them, Ty and Ben were walking slowly, their eyes trained on the ground, looking for seashells. Every now and then, one of them would find one, and hold it up for the other's inspection. They stayed close together, their hands occasionally bumping. I might be imagining it, but I thought Ben was making it happen more often than proximity could quite account for.

"You're right." I turned back to Nicky. He was grinning at me, and I figured he'd probably been following my eyes around the beach. "I'm good here. With all of you."

"Damn straight." Then he leaned over and kissed me, and any worries I'd had disappeared.

We got up and drifted from group to group for a while, looking for shells, playing Frisbee, chasing each other around the beach without caring what anyone thought, until the sun started to set. Ben had a permit to make a campfire, and he and Micah got it going.

Nick and I sat around it with everyone for a while. Tuck, Bellamy, and Ty had brought guitars, and they played, and almost everyone took a turn singing. Ava got excited and made everyone wait while she found sticks for her and Micah to bang against the lid of the cooler in time to the songs. She offered Nicky a pair, but he declined. He was lying back against me, his head on my shoulder, his eyes drifting closed while the music rose up around us.

I half thought he might fall asleep there, and I'd have to wake him up when it was time for us to go home. But after a few more songs, he sat up and turned to me, and held out his hand.

"Come with me?" he asked, soft enough that he wasn't interrupting the music.

I nodded and let him tug me up. We stepped away from the group. Micah smiled at me as we went, but no one commented or asked where we were headed.

It was dark away from the fire. I could see a couple of other flames, a ways down the beach, but in front of us, there was only a long strip of sand silvered by the moon, and the blackness of the waves.

Nick held my hand and pulled me until we were knee-deep in the water. We'd gone in earlier, jumping through the waves, splashing each other. It was different now, though. The water was cool, pushing around our legs, and I imagined there were all kinds of things swimming in it, right under the surface. Nick stood close, his toes touching mine, chest to chest with me.

I wrapped my arms around his waist. "What are we doing out here?"

He squashed himself against me, and gestured out at the water. His hand was a flicker of shadow against the ocean. "I wanted to see the moon on the water. It's pretty, right?" He took a deep breath. His back rose and fell under my palms. "We used to party on this beach when I was in high school. It was fun." He laughed quietly. "Lot of good times. But I used to . . . Sometimes I snuck away, in the middle of it all. I liked to see the water in the dark. It's not the same, right? It's like . . ." He sighed. "It's like all the mystery of it comes to the shore. And the moon on it . . . it looks like you could fall into it forever."

I nodded. It did. It scared me, in some ways. It seemed so vast like this. In the daylight, the rational part of my mind knew it ended, but in the dark, it was as if anything could be possible. As if worlds were colliding, as if this were a different space completely, as if anything could come up from the depths, because this wasn't quite the same ocean as before.

"And," Nicky said, pulling me back from my thoughts. "I always used to like to look back at the party. See it all small and contained, in a single glimpse." He turned us, gently, our feet shifting in the sand. Behind us, the campfire glowed. I could make out Bellamy's and Ava's faces, could see the firelight catching on Tuck's guitar, turning it burnished bronze. A thin thread of music floated to us on the breeze. I couldn't quite tell what it was.

We turned back to the ocean. We stood like that for a long time—pressed together, the waves lapping at our knees.

"We should bring Josh to the beach. Would he like it?" I asked.

Nick rested his face against my shoulder. "He loves it. He would love that. He'd have a blast."

I'd like it too, I was pretty sure. I could already picture them, Nicky and Josh together, gathering up shells or dashing through the surf. I could picture myself with them too. It was startlingly crystal clear. Josh handing me seashells, the two of us carefully deciding where to place them on a sandcastle. Nick laughing as he ran down to the surf, to get water so the sand would be the exact right consistency for shaping. It would be perfect, all of it.

"I really want to do that." I kissed the top of Nicky's head.

"Me too." He took a deep breath. He was quiet for a minute, but it seemed as if he was making up his mind to say something.

"I'm sorry about your brother, Quinn," he whispered, finally. "I wish I'd been able to meet him."

I nodded. It didn't sting as much, standing here with Nicky. Not as much as I'd have expected. It ached, like he'd touched a deep bruise. A tender spot that would never go away. And that was okay. I wanted it to hurt. I wanted it to be tender. But I wanted to be able to talk about Eric too.

"I do too."

"Would we have gotten along, you think?"

I laughed, trying to picture quiet, introverted Eric with boisterous, energetic Nicky. "He would have been completely bowled over by you. He wouldn't have known what to make of you." I hugged him tighter, kissed his hair, then the side of his face, his jaw. "He'd have liked you. He'd have liked who I am when I'm with you."

Nicky leaned back enough that he could stare at me, cup his hands around my face. He stroked his thumb over my cheekbone. "And who are you when you're with me?"

I sighed, like I was letting go of everything. "Somebody good. Somebody . . . somebody who knows who he is."

He smiled at me. His face was in shadow, his expression cast in darkness, but I could see the happiness on him. "That's good, then."

I huffed out a laugh. "Yeah. It is. It's very good."

I don't know which one of us leaned forward first, or if we both had the same idea at the same time. His lips were warm on mine, slightly chapped from the sun. I shivered from the sensation of it, our bodies hot against each other, warm skin on warm skin, except where the water was cool around our legs. I slid my hand up his neck, into his hair, held him to me, and he pressed against me. Twisted his arms around me. Opened his mouth to mine, skimmed his tongue over my lips, velvet soft. Kissed me deeply, as if there wasn't anyone on the beach but him and me. I held him even closer, impossibly close, wanting to lose all my senses in him. Kissed him harder. He tasted like sugar and seaweed and himself. Like sunlight and salt, and the smoke from the campfire.

He tasted like home.

Explore more of the *Escaping Indigo* series:
riptidepublishing.com/titles/series/escaping-indigo

Dear Reader,

Thank you for reading Eli Lang's *Scratch Track*!

We know your time is precious and you have many, many entertainment options, so it means a lot that you've chosen to spend your time reading. We really hope you enjoyed it.

We'd be honored if you'd consider posting a review—good or bad—on sites like **Amazon, Barnes & Noble, Kobo, Goodreads, Twitter, Facebook, Tumblr,** and your blog or website. We'd also be honored if you told your friends and family about this book. Word of mouth is a book's lifeblood!

For more information on upcoming releases, author interviews, blog tours, contests, giveaways, and more, please sign up for our weekly, spam-free newsletter and visit us around the web:

**Newsletter**: tinyurl.com/RiptideSignup
**Twitter**: twitter.com/RiptideBooks
**Facebook**: facebook.com/RiptidePublishing
**Goodreads**: tinyurl.com/RiptideOnGoodreads
**Tumblr**: riptidepublishing.tumblr.com

Thank you so much for Reading the Rainbow!

RiptidePublishing.com

# acknowledgments

Lots of thanks as always to my parents. Many, many thanks to Rain Merton, for writing side by side with me, being an incredible beta reader, talking me through revisions, and holding my hand while I panicked. You are amazing. Many thanks also to my editor, May Peterson, for such wonderful insights, being so patient with me, and helping me polish this into something way better than I had. And thanks to everyone else at Riptide for being so great. Lots of thanks to Ryan for all the studio and drumming knowledge (anything that's wrong is totally all me), and for being an awesome friend. And many thanks to all the Blanketeers for being the best and always coming to the rescue when I need you. You are the most wonderful people.

ALSO BY
# eli lang

*Escaping Indigo series*
Escaping Indigo
Skin Hunger

Half

# ABOUT
# the author

Eli Lang is a writer and drummer. She's played in rock bands, worked on horse farms, and had jobs in libraries, where she spent most of her time reading every book she could get her hands on. She can fold a nearly perfect paper crane and knows how to tune a snare drum. She still buys stuffed animals because she feels bad if they're left alone in the store, believes cinnamon buns should always be eaten warm, can tell you more than you ever wanted to know about the tardigrade, and has a book collection that's reaching frightening proportions. She lives in Arizona with far too many pets.

Website: leftoversushi.com
Facebook: facebook.com/EliLangAuthor
Twitter: twitter.com/eli__lang
Goodreads: goodreads.com/eli_lang